The Nameless

II: The Last Brawl

BELLAVISTA

II

The Last Brawl

The Nameless II: The Last Brawl

Introduction

Earth. Today, the Night sky was something very special. Thousands of small sparkling stars filled the vastness black cloth. Some shone like rubies, others looked rather dull. Countless human eyes looked up at the sky in the warm spring night and enjoyed this sight. Some dreamed of something. Maybe of happiness for two, or of a house, a lot of money and a fast car. Dreams that one day might come true or not.

In any case, people enjoyed this nocturnal moment. Everything was so peaceful and quiet. But this could change, because nobody knows what the future awaits every one of them.

Chapter 1

Marblehead, Massachusetts, U.S.A. It was one of the oldest fishing ports in New England. Founded in 1633, the community is now a distinguished suburb of Boston on the Atlantic Ocean. Further away from the sheltered harbor, a small residential area can be found in a quiet suburb. It was a small area; thus, they know every single one and would greet each other every time. Everyone had a good relationship with one another. The world seemed to be still at this place.

A little high up on a small hill, one house stood. A family of five lives here. That night, the master of the house slept very restlessly. Sweat beads had formed on his forehead and he moved his head from right to left, agitated. The pajamas he was wearing had absorbed his bodily sweat. He moaned and moaned, but after a while, he slept gently like an infant. The wife next to him awoke and was worried. She wanted to wake up her husband. But she let it go when she noticed that he calmed down again. Knowing that her husband's nightmare must have ended, she went back to sleep.

Chapter 2

Northern Norway. The town of *Tromsø*, with its 77,000 inhabitants, was situated in *Balsfjord*. With a width of 2,558*km2*, it is Norway's largest municipality. The *Eismeerkathedrale* was the landmark of this town and stood high in front of the high bridge that led to the fjord island. In Tromsø, there were a few streets next to the Polar Institute, the Main University and the University's Museum. Jan Karlesson grew up in Tromsø. From an early age, he wanted to know everything about the country's history. Jumping from one university to another, he learned everything he could about indigenously people, including their buildings and land usage. With his expertise in a lot of fields, he easily became internationally-known. Some national governments around the globe would keep asking him for advice when they didn't know what to do.

One day, an offer came from overseas. It was about the management of a university. He felt flattered, but he politely declined. Jan had reasons for that. First, he was already appointed as the director of Tromsø University. Second, Tromsø University was being rebuilt and enlarged with renovations and a new hall was being built. A special hall for an unusual object. The money was entirely paid by the government. Karlesson had to supervise everything. It was a lot of work. He barely had chance to enjoy his coffee in peace. One morning came, Jan Karlesson was arriving in his office when he found a letter from the government. He was curious so he picked it up and read it. When he finished reading the letter, his heart made a leap of joy. "This is unbelievable," he whispered to himself.

Chapter 3

25 years later. It was shortly after 20:07 in the evening, when Jan Karlesson, who was now 65 years old, walked down the staircase. He was the last to leave the university. He wanted to take the folder full of documents home and study it there. Karlesson also wanted to enjoy his well-deserved long weekend. He walked through the halls and approached the exit door when he felt a breath of wind. *'Strange. I know I closed all the windows,'* he thought. He wanted to get to the bottom of this.

He put the folder on the ground and turned to the right. Then he stepped off. It was the direction where the attached hall was. Suddenly, he froze. It was a cold breath that hit him. *"Brr!"* he reacted. He reached the entrance door of the hall. It was locked. He fingered a bunch of keys out of his pocket and put the key into the lock. By turning it to the right, the door was no longer locked. Jan Karlesson had a bad feeling about opening the door. But he wanted to see if the cold breeze came from here. Slowly, he pushed the door handle down and pulled the door towards him. Despite the poor lighting, he saw everything in the room. It drove through his body. The bad feeling became fear. He had never seen anything like it before. He bounced back and screamed out his fear. Then, he fell to the ground and a deep impotence lay over him.

Chapter 4

The night watchman Olsson found the helpless director half an hour later, when he made his rounds. He shouted, "Sir Jan!" to the motionless man and ran to him. He knelt to the ground and looked at him. The director's face was pale.

The night watchman whispered, "My goodness!" He stood up and ran to the bathrooms. There he fetched a wet cloth and dabbed the director's face with it, moments later. He opened his eyes blinking and recognized the night watchman.

"Are you alright, Sir?" he asked.

The director spoke with a cawing voice, "Quick, lock the door. Quickly!"

Olsson turned around and locked the door to the hall. Meanwhile, Jan Karlsson straightened up and said, "No one is allowed to be in this hall. Nobody. You understand?"

Then, he walked away with shaky legs and informed his superiors. Olsson looked after him and shook his head. "What has gotten into him?" he said to himself. Then he turned to the door. "What does all this mean?" He pulled his shoulders up and continued with his routine check walks.

Chapter 5

Friday morning came and with it, the chirping of the birds. The man woke up and looked on the left side of his bed. It looked empty. His wife had already gotten up. *'She's probably in the kitchen making breakfast,'* he thought and got up, too.

His pajamas felt wet and cold in some places. His sweat had cooled down. He went into the bathroom and slipped into the shower. As soon as he was finished, he went into the bedroom and covered himself with the clothes of the day. A delicious scent filled up his nose.

"Hmm-mm! That smells good," he said to himself.

The smell of breakfast filled the house. He went down the stairs in a rush. In the lower part of the house were the living room and the kitchen. On the adjacent side, the doors to the garage and the cellar. In the upper floor, there were the bedrooms and the bathrooms of the family. The man entered the kitchen and saw the breakfast table as always. With a warm "Good Morning, everyone" he greeted his family, who were already at the table.

"Good morning, Dad," the three young adults addressed the father.

Mikael was the oldest at the age of 24. Then Andy came at the age of 22 and finally, Irina at the age of 19. The man went to his wife and breathed a kiss on her forehead.

He whispered, "I love you," in her right ear.

"Oh, my love, I know that," she gave back. "I love you too."

The man took a seat on his chair. After the morning prayers, he gave only two words from himself, "Free breakfast. "

During the meal, the daily routine was discussed. "Today is the last working day before us. It will be hard. The ship delivery from Scandinavia will arrive at the port in less than two hours. Mikael, you will coordinate the process as discussed. See to it that nothing breaks apart. Andy and I will inspect the camps and prepare the goods for the next days. Irina, you will cooperate with the truck drivers and load the goods. You leave the heavy things to the truck drivers and the warehouse staff. Make sure everything runs smoothly."

"Yes, Dad," the three young adults answered with an evident hint of boredom.

"It's not the first time, isn't it?" said Mikael.

"Not even the second time," Irina added.

"It's the third time already. Or were there several times before?" Andy gave off himself.

"Now would you listen to this gang," the head of the house

said of himself and looked at his wife looking for help.

"You don't have to look at me like that. You have also raised this gang."

"But they got that from you."

"Oh, so they did. They are, dear, your children, too. And if not, they're just all mine then?"

"No. No, I didn't mean it that way, although...,"

"What then?" said the woman.

He gave back, "Nothing, nothing," with a smile.

"*Hah!*" the wife said, "You wanted to annoy me again and take me in for a ride!"

"That's what I had in mind, though I only partly succeeded."

Three quarters of an hour later, the three young adults were on their way to the harbor. The man stayed at home for a while because he still wanted to help his wife. He put the dishes in the dishwasher while the wife vacuumed the bedroom. Then she went back downstairs. The shopping list had been made. Her next goal was shopping. She went into the kitchen, where the husband sat on a chair and breathed deeply. When she saw him like that, she was startled.

"Darling! What 's wrong? Don't you feel well?"

"I don't know. Something's bothering me," he said.

"What is it? Does it have something to do with your dream last night?"

"What do you mean?"

"I woke up in the middle of the night, and looked at you. You had beads of sweat on your forehead and moaned loudly. I was worried. But you calmed down and carried on sleeping, so I didn't bother waking you up."

"Did I? Did I sleep badly?"

"Yes!"

"Then it has to do with the strange dream."

"What kind of dream is it?" she asked.

"I don't know. I can't figure it out. That's why it's bothering me. I dreamt about weird stuff."

The wife asked "Tell me everything."

"Well. I remember I came out of the darkness into a diffused light. It wasn't very bright. Fog was all around me. I walked through the fog and pushed my foot against a stone step that led upstairs. I took one step after the other, and a lot of time passed. But I suspected that time was not relevant there. The fog lifted. At first, I did not know what I saw. Only contours of something I could not vividly see. It looked like a post. There was something attached to it. I could not see it. Then, I heard a powerful voice that made me shiver. The voice said, *'Every mortal who dares cross the bridge must die. I am the guardian. Come closer and you will face death'.* I was frightened like never before in my life. But then, I felt that I didn't have to be afraid. Thus, I took a step forward and the dream stopped there."

The wife spoke, "That's a really strange dream."

"I found that strange as well. What could this mean?" the man asked helplessly.

"I don't know. But let us wait and see. Maybe everything will clear up some time."

"You're always right. If I did not have you then...," the man spoke and stood up. He hugged his wife and gave her a kiss.

"Then, you would have someone else as your wife."

"No, certainly not. I fell in love with you right then and there when we first met, remember?"

"Yes, I know how it all began. It was a terrible time, but you still pursued me after all that." His wife giggled.

Both knew what obstacles they had been through. These were beautiful, but also incredibly dangerous when they met for the first time. He loosened his embrace and said, "But now it's time to go. We still have the weekend ahead of us. Then, we can go on our holiday." The two said their goodbyes.

He went to the shop and she went shopping.

Chapter 6

New Mexico. Three and a half months later. An establishment called S.E.T.I. was the center of research for the search for extraterrestrial life forms. In front of the building, stood countless parabolic mirrors called radio telescopes, which were always ready to capture signals from space. It was 02:27 on a Saturday morning. Expensive and complicated devices stood around in the center. Tom Daily sat at the table and read a copy of the Playboy magazine. His pointed nose almost pierced the notebook. The glasses on his nose sat a little crooked. Apparently, he liked the article on the double page.

"Not to be grasped. Oh...wow," he spoke to himself.

He took it easy because there was nothing going on tonight. Time did not seem to pass. The minutes stretched length. In between, he looked at the screens. They showed a horizontal line from left to right. From one second to the next, the lines on the screen made waves.

"T-there's no such thing–What the," stammered Tom Daily. The magazine flew to the side, and he concentrated on the screen. "Sorry, baby," he said, "but duty calls."

He briefly peered over to Playboy, who was lying somewhere in the corner. Tom believed this was a mistake. He had never seen anything like it before. With fast fingers, he pressed countless buttons on the switch console. On the screen, the waves were zigzagging back and forth. This was much stronger than before. Tom Daily sounded the alarm. In this station, there were dormitories. Somebody was always readily there when a connection is picked up.

After a few minutes, the station manager met Tom Daily and rubbed his eyes. He looked quite tired. But when Tom Daily spoke to him, the tiredness left his soul.

"Sir! We're picking up a signal. A very strong signal."

"I see it. Have you located it's origin yet?"

"No. Not yet. It seems to me it's coming from all sides. I don't understand."

"Have you been able to locate the distance of the signal?"

"No. A moment, please."

Tom Daily pressed a button and typed codes on the keyboard with fast finger strokes. After pressing the Enter key, the computer calculated the distance. "Why is it taking so long?" Tom said nervously.

"Patience, young man," said the superior. Something flickered across the screen. It was the data. "That's just a signal from Mars," said the station manager a little disappointed.

"No, Sir. Far more than that. Look! It shows a farther distance," said Tom Daily.

"It's from farther away than I thought. But from where exactly?"

At that moment, the power suddenly went out. The room was in full darkness. Only one screen remained on line. It was the computer that was connected to the signal. Confused, the two men looked at each other.

"What's going on here?" whispered the station manager.

Tom Daily pressed some buttons. Nothing happened. It was like some power had shut everything down. Only one screen stayed on. Suddenly, something unexpected happened. The picture, where the waves were before, disappeared. A flickering picture appeared, like the end of a TV channel. It roared. Something emerged from the flickering picture. A very weak contour had formed. The two men looked spellbound at the flicker box.

"It's out of focus," whispered Tom Daily.

The other one said, "Never mind."

"There, look". He pointed his finger at the screen.

Shortly before the picture returned to its original state, the men heard a deep hissing voice, "*This time, you will all die. I will destroy you all.*"

The room and the equipment regained power again.

Everything went as if nothing had happened. The two men looked at each other. No one had a healthy complexion anymore. They looked pale white, as if all their blood had been taken.

"What was that?" whispered Tom Daily.

"I don't know, but I have a hunch."

"What kind?"

"It's more of a hunch and a bad feeling. It reminds me of something that had happened over 25 years ago."

"What kind of thing?" asked Tom Daily.

"A dangerously terrible thing. Excuse me. I have to make a phone call." He left the room and went to the phone. There he typed in a number only he knew. After a few seconds, someone picked up the phone at the other end. "CODE 12.7.5. This is Jack Clark. Sorry to disturb you at night, Sir. But something had happened."
Later, he deleted the number again so that nobody could operate the recall button.

Chapter 7

Washington D.C. Saturday. 11:44 AM. A heavy limousine drove up the road to the White House. The car stopped and a general got out. With swift marches, he moved towards the entrance. The door was opened for him, and a security guard accompanied him inside the house. Security guards stood around everywhere, radioing everything that was inside the building. The general was taken directly to the President's study. The door was already open. He entered, and the door was closed behind him.

"Come closer, General. Take a seat, please," the President said. The highest man of the nation stood up from his leather armchair behind the desk, approached the general and shook his hand. The two took a seat on the cream-colored couch. "How bad is it?" asked the President.

"I can't precisely say yet, Mr. President. But I suspect it might get worse than it did 25 years ago."

"What can we do?"

"I suggest we start the red alert. Then activate the various telecommunications satellites."

"But the satellites are only good for transmissions, right?"

"That's not the case, Sir. When we solved the problem here on earth years ago, the former President took precautions. He had satellites made from taxpayers' money. Just in case something similar to what happened 25 years ago would happen again. It is believed that it is normal to shoot up telecommunication satellites so that we would have better reception on Earth. That is what the population are meant to believe. But these satellites are camouflaged. They are equipped with special nuclear weapons."

"What are you saying? Why wasn't I informed until now?"

"You'll have to ask the former President, Sir. All I know is that this is appropriate for such an emergency. You see, Sir, science has made great progress in those recent years. Nuclear weapons are only intended for space. If they are fired from Earth, they will explode shortly after launch. Even if only one of them should have a malfunction, it will not be a problem. It would burn up in the atmosphere. You see, Sir, everything is in order."

"Are you kidding me, General? There's nothing wrong here. This will have repercussions for whoever is responsible for it."

"If we get to that. The signals would have become much stronger. I'm afraid it won't be long before we can see something on our screens."

"Well, do everything you need to do. Give a silent alarm. The population must not be informed under any circumstances. Before you go, General, I expect you to keep me informed." The two of them stood up and shook hands. "Goodbye, General," the President said.

"Sir, I have something personal on my mind. May I speak freely?"

"Yes. What is it?"

"There will be a meeting at the Ministry of Defense. However, I will not be present."

"Why not?"

"I would like to seek the advice of a civilian. He was the one who helped us back then. If possible, if he agrees to help, I want him by my side."

The President was silent for a moment. "Can you trust this man? Will he be silent when he sees all the secrets of the military?" asked the President.

"Sir," the general stood tight and greeted. "I would entrust my life to this man. He saved my life back then."

"Alright. Do whatever you have to do."

The general moved out of the room. The President stepped towards his desk and pressed a button on the desk telephone.

"Yes, Mr. President?" it came out of the loudspeaker.

"Miss Johnson. Call in James Bloom, please."

Meanwhile, the General left the White House and got into the car. He reached for the phone. A female voice answered on the other side.

"Yes, Sir?"

"Alice, we have a red alert. You know what to do."

Then he hung up. His gaze wandered to the right to the side seat. Some files were there. One of them had S.E.T.I. written on it. He had received this file recently. On the other file, Norway was written and on the third, there was no title. The general knew what was in the unnamed file. He picked it up and bobbed it up and down. Then he put it back in the other files. He looked to the left at the inside of the car doors. There were some buttons. He pressed one of these buttons and the connecting disc between him and the driver lowered.

He said, "Mr. Dumbler, please drive me to the military airport. The plane is waiting for us."

"Where is General going this time?" asked the driver.

"To Marblehead, Massachusetts."

Chapter 8

The Army headquarters was like a madhouse. The news of the general had set the military machinery in motion. The other states were also informed in secrecy. Within 24 hours, everyone was ready to sacrifice their lives for the Earth.

Chapter 9

The danger came from outer space. There was a semi-dark room in the approaching spaceship. There was a fearsome creature inside. It was difficult to see its contours.

"What does it look like with the other combat ships?" hissed the voice out of the room.

Another malicious voice answered from a room next door, "They all came from the other side at the same time. Soon, we will have contact with this little planet again."

The voice hissed. "Good. This time no one will stop me from killing those low-life creatures."

Chapter 10

Saturday afternoon. It was about 15:27 PM when the military plane landed at the indicated base. The general and the driver got off the plane. A black limousine stood ready.

"Let's drive, Mr. Dumbler. You know the way," said the general.

"Yes, Sir, no problem with the navigation system."

"Well, go ahead and turn on the air conditioning. It's hotter here than in Washington D.C."

"Yes, Sir."

The driver opened the door for the general. As soon as he sat in it, Mr. Dumbler sat behind the wheel. Someone had entered the destination data beforehand. Mr. Dumbler started the car and drove off.

Chapter 11

Saturday at 16:14PM. The family of five was at home. The woman was standing in the kitchen while the others were at the pool. The sun was shining and everyone was in a good mood. They were rare moments, as everyone had little time for themselves. Everyone worked their own businesses. Of course, only the two young men were full-time employees. Irina, the daughter, did this part-time because she still went to school and will graduate in the next month. No one thought at that moment that her life would change. This began when the doorbell rang.

When the woman heard the doorbell, she shouted outside, "I'm coming!" The rest of the family heard this.

"Who can bother us on our weekend?" Irina said. She lolled on the sun lounger.

"Someone who got lost, perhaps," said the father. The two sons swam their rounds in the pool.

"He can experience something new," said Mikael.

"Experience what?" Andy added his mustard.

"Let's get the buttons in front of us."

Both wanted to get out of the water, but the father held them back.

"You stay where you are. Your mother will be able to cope with it."

In the meantime, the woman approached the front door. She held a towel in her fingers and wiped her wet hands. She pushed the door handle down and opened the front door. A man in a driver's uniform stood in front of the door.

"Who is it?"

"I'm sorry to bother you, Mrs. Fenton. The General would like to speak to your husband." He cleared the way.

The woman could see the man coming up the stairs. She was a little frightened.

"My God," she whispered.

"Hello, Mrs. Fenton. How are you?"

"Sergeant Rock. Pardon me, I meant General Rock." She gave him the still wet hand. "Please come in."

"Thank you." He entered and stopped.

"And Mister Driver?" she asked.

The general didn't have to say anything. The driver turned around and walked back to the car. *'This will take a long time,'*

Mr. Dumbler thought and a short time later, he read a newspaper in the limousine.

The general stopped in the entrance hall.

The woman said, "Follow me into the living room, please," and walked to the right. "I will fetch my husband. Please take a seat on the sofa."

"Thank you," spoke General Rock. He had clamped his cap under his right arm. He held the files in his right hand.

Meanwhile, Helen Fenton walked to the pool. The man saw his wife approaching. Her face, unreadable. His face darkened. He suspected something was wrong. "What's the matter, Helen?" he asked worriedly.

"It's better if you put something on. We have a visitor. I don't think it's anything to be happy about."

"Who came?"

"General Rock. He used to be a Sergeant. You remember?"

"How can I forget? I'll be right there."

He got up, put on the short cotton trousers and the cotton T-shirt and walked towards the house with Helen. Both disappeared through the door to the living room.

Chapter 12

The three young adults had only partially learned who had come. Their reactions were corresponding. They pulled their shoulders up. No one knew what it was all about. The two boys came out of the pool and dried quickly. Irina put on some clothes and waited for her brothers.

"Quick," she whispered, "I don't want to miss anything."

"Yes, all right. We're coming," Andy said.

The two young men put on their trousers. On their toes, they stepped towards the door, then to the right through the kitchen door. They opened them silently and penetrated the inside of the house. From there to the left, through the entrance hall and stopped behind the corner of the wall. They listened to the men.

Chapter 13

General Rock. What a surprise," Erik Fenton stepped up to the man and shook his hand. The general, who had got up again, returned the handshake. "It's been a long time since we last saw each other."

"Yes, Mr. Fenton, and I apologize very much for this disturbance."

"Don't bother about it. But please, do sit down," said Erik Fenton and pointed to the couch.

"Thank you."

"Would you like something to drink?" asked Helen Fenton.

"Gladly. A mineral water would be ideal."

Helen Fenton walked to the house bar and came back with a mineral bottle and three glasses. She placed it on the salon table and poured it in.

Helen asked, "How are you?"

"As you can see, I have a few more military degrees hanging from my jacket. This military career has opened some doors for me since General Cobe passed away. I climbed up. I met the woman of my life almost twenty years ago and got married. I have two children. They are studying and want to become lawyers."

"I'm happy for you, General," said Erik Fenton. "But what does your presence give us?"

"More than just a courtesy visit. Knowing you well, Mr. Fenton, you like it the quick and direct way."

"That's correct. Tell me, General."

"I don't even know where to start."

"It's best not to start yet," said Erik Fenton. He spoke to the entrance hall. "You can come out, kids. I know you're listening." One by one, they showed themselves to the guest. "These are our children," said Erik Fenton. "The oldest is Mikael. Then comes Andy and finally Irina."

The General rose and greeted the three. Then he sat down again. The young people stood in the room, embarrassed and caught, looking at their parents.

"How did you know we were listening, father?" Andy asked.

"I heard nothing from the pool and connected the dots. You could only hide behind the wall. It's the only point where you can listen well."

"Blimey, how can he do that? How does he always know a lot in advance?" asked Mikael.

"Because he is our father. That's why," Irina said.

"Exactly," was Helen Fenton's message. "Because he is your father and knows exactly what you are planning next. You are our only children. Now leave. We have something important to discuss with the General."

Irina asked, "Can't we stay?"

"No."

"Why not? After all, we want to know why a general shows up here, even though Dad never had anything to do with the military," Mikael said.

"You heard what your mother said," said Erik Fenton, firmly.

"But–."

"No buts. Now Go!" Erik's voice had an annoyed tone, and the three only knew what it meant.

General Rock was silent. But here he spoke to Erik Fenton. "Mr. Fenton. With all due respect. I believe it is necessary that your children stay here. Actually, it concerns them too."

Surprised, the parents looked at the general. "What do you mean?"

"Do your children know of the incident of York?" he whispered.

"No," gave Erik Fenton back.

"But they should. Because we are facing a possible bigger problem that affects the nation and the rest of the world."

"What?! What are you saying?" Erik Fenton gave up and jumped up.

The children retreated. They had never seen their father like that before. It seemed as if he didn't have any tiredness for his old age. That was strange. Helen Fenton was frightened and held her hand in front of her mouth.

"Mr. Fenton, please," said General Rock.

Erik Fenton sat down again. "Now don't make it so surprising, general. Say what you have to say," Erik Fenton asked the general.

"The military has prepared files on the incident that occurred. One about you, among other things. I studied it in detail. You have come a long way. You founded a small company and today, you own a few shops in every state. You are well-known and a rich man Mr. Fenton. Not only with the population, which you supply with exclusive specialties from Scandinavia, but also with the military. They think you are a very brave man. Those who were there then think a lot of you. I'm one of them. Be that as it may. I don't want to gloss over anything, but I suspect that our world as we know it will soon be gone. Your house, your existence, everything is threatened again. That is what I wanted to tell you. Please forgive me." His voice went down.

The family was shocked. Nobody spoke a word. Time ran by.

The young people, who were still a little wet, almost froze to death. They trembled all over. Helen Fenton still closed his mouth with her hand, according to the words of the general. Erik Fenton cleared his throat before saying anything again.

"What's the matter? What happened?" He had recovered quickly and seemed sober.

The general noticed that. "First, I must have an oath from your children. A vow of silence. Nothing may penetrate outside. No matter what I say. I entrust that your children will keep their word."

Irina was close to tears. "What is it, Dad? Why does this man come to us and tell us such horrible things? I am afraid. Tell him to go away. Please, Dad."

"Irina. I can't, and I don't want to, because I want to know what's going on. Besides, I made my promise not to tell anyone. The same applies to your mother. We can be silent. We have done that for many years. I ask and expect you three to do the same."

The three children looked at each other for a few seconds. They sighed and hesitantly agreed. But before the General could speak any further, the three wanted to put on something else. Hastily and with quick steps, they disappeared into their rooms and returned with other clothes on their bodies.

Meanwhile, the general drank the cool water out of the glass. The family was completely gathered in the living room and listened eagerly to the General's words. "Well, as I said, I don't know where to start. But it would be best if I started three and a half months ago." He pointed to one of the files on the salon table.

"What happened?" asked Erik Fenton.

"Something extraordinary. It happened in the night of Thursday to Friday."

"My God," said Helen Fenton in horror. "Erik, do you remember?"

"How can I forget?"

"What's going on? What do you have?" Asked the general.

"My husband had a strange dream last night."

"What kind of dream was it?" The General asked Fenton.

"I don't know exactly what it was. I walked through fog. Then, I pushed with my foot against stone steps. I walked up these, and a voice warned me not to go any farther."

"What did they say?" the general asked.

"Every mortal who dares cross the bridge must die. I am the guardian. Come closer and face death."

"Unbelievable," said General Rock. "Somehow I suspect there is more to this dream and it is connected with my report." The general took a sip of water.

Erik Fenton looked at his wife. She also did not know what's going to come now. The three young adults sat still. Everything was new for them. No one knew exactly what it was.

"Do you remember the Drakkar?" General Rock started the report. He pointed to the other file.

"Of course. I was there. Does it have anything to do with it?"

"I think so. The night you had your strange dream, the Drakkar was active."

"My God," spoke Erik.

"What's wrong? How are you feeling?" asked Helen.

Erik got up, slowly walked to the window, and looked out. The rest of the people saw his back. Then they heard his voice. "I have tried to forget. To repress everything. But the past catches up with me today. You, who knew everything, know what I'm talking about." He turned around. "General," he looked at the man. "Is it possible that today you want to tell me about a higher power? A dangerous power?"

"Yes."

"Damn," Erik Fenton cursed himself. His children had never seen or heard him like that. "I always had the feeling that it wasn't completely over." Erik Fenton took a short break before he continued, "IT is still in me. Only IT never activated, until the night I had the dream. It wanted to tell me something, that's for sure. I still don't know what it is." He walked back to the couch, let himself plop in and took a long sip of water.

His wife held him by the arm. She was worried. "Erik," she said. "You never told me about this. Why? Don't you trust me?"

"No. No. I didn't want to frighten you. I had to fight it out alone."

"I understand, father," Mikael interrupted the silence that had spread in the living room. "What is this IT you're referring to?" he wanted to know.

Erik had calmed down and spoke to his children. "At that time, I didn't know who my father was. It was only by chance that I met him and lost him right after. He died after I had been with him. It was at that moment when the problems began. The power he carried within him passed over to me. The Nameless one called himself IT. I was guilty of summoning death and destruction. When I found out why he was on earth, I wanted to quit my job and do something simple. Which I did later. It was at that time that I met your mother. I don't want to say any more about it. It was already difficult enough to forget the events of that time. Especially for your mother. IT is a being from another world. An alien, as you would say. I carried IT inside me."

That was like a hammer blow to the face for Erik's children. Silence spread until Irina broke through the silence. "What's this weird story? How did it go on?"

"I'll tell you that some other time. What's important now is what's coming. Please, General, continue with your story."

"Well, I have to give it a rest. At that time, the Norwegian Military Air Force picked you up with two helicopters. But what you didn't know was that General Cobe sent me and some men to look for the Drakkar. Via the Interstellar satellite, we could locate the ship. With some strong helicopters, we made ourselves on our way. A few hours passed till we discovered the ship on the open sea. We flew towards the Drakkar and my men, as well as I, jumped into the ice-cold floods. Of course, the diving suit protected us. With a few swimming movements, we reached the ship and boarded. The sail was still taut and a light wind blew it up. One of my men stepped to the rudder and turned the ship towards home. But we did not get far. The Norwegian Navy put a spoke in our wheel. With a warship and two frigates, they approached us. We had to leave the ship to the Norwegians in order to avoid a political conflict. After all, it belonged to those people. The ship was later taken to Tromsø in northern Norway. A new hall was built at the university next to the museum. There, the ship remained and everybody could see it for a whole 25 years. Everything was fine until a few months ago.

That evening, the Drakkar was active. Jan Karlsson, the university professor, went inside the hall and fainted when he saw what was going on." General Rock took a little sip of water before continuing. "The professor looked at the ship. From front to back, the faces were imprinted in the wood. You know them, don't you, Mr. Fenton?" Erik Fenton was silent, but his head nodded slightly. "Something was wrong with the faces. Your face in the wood was surrounded by a bright aura that slowly disappeared. What made the professor shiver was the first face. The face of Erik, the Viking. It was surrounded by a foggy darkness. He had opened his mouth wide and screamed his pain out. Of course, this scream was inaudible, but his features said it all. His face changed to a spongy mass. The dark mist lay on his face. Then, the fog disappeared and along with it, the face of Erik, the Viking. What remained was an empty area on the railing. Jan Karlsson immediately reported the incident to the local authorities. This information reached us as well as the other thing that happened the same evening."

"What thing?" asked Erik Fenton. Like the other members of his family, he was anxious to see what would happen next.

General Rock pointed to the other file on the salon table. "S.E.T.I. had contact," were his words. "In the headquarters, the power went out. Nothing worked. Absolute darkness, except a screen. A computer screen that can't show or transmit pictures at all. The picture flickered like the end of a TV program. In this flicker, a weak contour of a being was created. It threatened to destroy us. Then the light came back and everything went on as if nothing had happened. The responsible manager of the station called me in the middle of the night and informed me. After I had all data and information from the two most different places with me, I could inform the President. So was the National Security Department. We are on red alert as we're speaking." General Rock stopped. He let his words fade away in the room.

The family almost stopped their breath at this terrible report. The family's throats had dried out. They drank the mineral water hastily. No one spoke a word. Everyone waited for some sign from the head of the house. Erik's thoughts were confused. 'What is going on here?' was his thought. But he could not give an exact resolution of this unbelievable thing. He just looked at General Rock. "That's unbelievable," he whispered. "What is brewing there?"

"Possibly the end," said the general. "The nation and the rest of the world are ready to fight. It's a fight for the earth and for humanity."

The family was silent. No one spoke a word. The young adults were pale and so was Helen Fenton. Only Erik remained calm before addressing the General. "Who can harm us? Who is it?"

"I don't know. What we do know is that whoever was contour on the screen threatened to destroy us. It said, 'this time you will die'," the general said.

Erik stood up and walked slowly. "Hmm! Have you already thought about why this thing uttered these words in our language?"

The general shook his head. "No, I have no answer!"

"Me, neither. But I have a guess. But this is impossible."

"Just say it."

"I am talking here about something or someone who must have been here on earth a long time ago. It said, this time you will die. So, we did something to this 'thing' once. But when exactly this was, I don't know. I am not sure yet. Maybe I'll find out more once I do my research. For it cannot be such coincidences that so many strange occurrences would follow each other."

"Yes, perhaps," the general said. "Or," he truncated, "it has something to do with the Nameless."

"I've thought of that," Erik Fenton said. "Everything is possible. But what does the strange dream have to do with me?" Erik Fenton walked to the window and looked out. His gaze darkened. 'Was this The End?' he thought.

"Mr. Fenton," said the general. "I had hoped that you would give me some advice or help me solve this riddle. But I see that we are not getting any further at the moment."

"What do you suggest, General?" asked Erik.

"The situation is serious. That's why I took measures. I want your family to come with me. We will take you to a safe place. Because I suspect that the alien power will be after you, Mr. Fenton. I'm sure you see it that way, don't you?"

Erik Fenton thought about it briefly and spoke to his family. "The general is right. I already had that thought. It is better if you go with the general."

Erik's children shouted, "No! We won't leave you, father!" They jumped up.

Helen Fenton also rose from the couch and looked at Erik. She looked into his eyes and immediately spoke to her children. "Your father is right. Even if I am reluctant to do so, we must act. I believe that we only have a chance to survive if we go."

"But, mother..." Mikael said, "You want to leave our father here? Just like that?"

"It is the best for us. Your father can help himself. He knows what to do. Is it not like that, dear?" She looked at Erik. She knew this profound look.

"Your mother is right. I will possibly be the target of this strange power. I will face them. Alone! Now go into your rooms and take the most necessary clothes with you."

"But..." Andy wanted to say, but Erik's look didn't promise anything good. The three turned around and wanted to go into their rooms when a sight happened. They heard their mother scream.

"Erik!" pushed the woman away.

Hastily, the people turned around and saw the unbelievable. Erik Fenton hovered about 10 centimeters above the ground. His figure was enveloped in a bright light.

General and Helen Fenton wanted to see him, but he raised his left arm and showed his palm. It was a stop signal. "No, don't come any closer," he said. "Don't touch me. No matter what happens, go with the general. Including you, beloved woman. Now go!" His words echoed. Then he fell to the ground and remained lying. Erik had fainted. Nobody knew how long this lasted.

Chapter 14

Space. The spacecraft continued to approach Earth. From the inside, the being spoke to the other, "I locate a signal from the approaching planet. It is weak, but noticeable enough."

"Yes," hissed the evil leader from the other room. "I also see it on my screen. But it's not a signal. It's the same power I carry inside me. It took a long time for it to reactivate itself."

"The Force," it came from the half dark room.

"Yes, it is my reviled brother. But this time, he cannot escape me. We are all strong enough to destroy him. Then, the planet and the rest of the galaxy will truly belong to me." Full of hatred, the horrible creature made a hissing sound.

Chapter 15

The Nameless Is back,' were Erik's thoughts before he fell to the ground and fainted. *'He didn't leave me like he said at the time. But what is he up to now?'*

Erik saw himself lying on the ground. His spirit detached itself from his body and floated to the ceiling. From above, he saw his family with frightened faces. They spoke to each other, but he did not understand them. Then they stepped away, as he had told them. He was alone in the living room. His spirit floated higher up and broke through the living room ceiling. As soon as he had overcome it, it became dark before his eyes. He only saw darkness descending over him.

Chapter 16

The Fenton family stood around Erik. The general said to those present, "I will have you taken to a safe place now."

"No, we'll stay with our father," said Mikael. "We will not abandon him."

"You heard what your father said," Helen Fenton spoke seriously. "And that's exactly what we're going to do. It is for our safety. Go into your rooms and quickly pack some clothes. Then we will be off."

The three left the living room. A short time later, they reappeared at the front door.

In the meantime, the general spoke with Helen Fenton. "Mr. Dumbler, my driver, will take you and your children to a safe place. It's secret and I can't tell them where it is. When this is all over, I'll get back to you."

"What about you, General? Aren't you coming with us?"

"No. I'll stay here and take care of your husband. I owe him that."

"Then I won't go with my kids. I'll stay here too."

"No. You have to stay with your children. I beg you. From the way it looks right now, nobody can help your husband and we don't know what is coming. It's better if I stay instead of you."

Helen Fenton just nodded.

"You are right. Stay. You can certainly set something in motion faster than I can. But I would like you to inform me immediately, even if it is only the slightest change in my husband. Do you understand, General Rock?"

"Understood and promised Mrs. Fenton," was what the high-ranking general said.

Helen went to the bedroom. It looked so empty. No Erik nearby. Secretly, she cried. The look before, of her husband lying on the ground, pressed her tear glands. She felt so helpless.

She breathed deeply, calmed herself forcibly, and packed the most necessary things into a bag. As she walked to the front door, she saw her children standing in front of her.

"Let's go, children," she said sadly.

The family left the house. The driver, Mr. Dumbler, stood by the limousine and held the car doors open. He had already been informed by the general. "Madam, I am your driver. I ask all of you to get inside."

The family got in and the car doors closed.

"Isn't the general coming?" Andy asked.

"No, he stays with your father. He will inform us if anything changes," said Helen Fenton.

The limousine left the property and headed towards an unknown destination.

Chapter 17

The general slowly walked through the living room. Erik Fenton lay on the cool floor, motionless. His figure still shone brightly. The general had seen such a glow before. That was 25 years ago, when Erik and the horde of Vikings brought death to the extraterrestrials. The general turned over the couch so he could look at the man lying on the ground. Then he took a mineral bottle from the kitchen, sat down on the couch and opened the bottle. A hissing could be heard. The carbonic acid shot up and countless bubbles filled the bottle. He took a sip from the bottle. Then he put it on the table and opened his military jacket. He made himself comfortable on the couch, although he expected a change at any moment. This did not happen. Thus, the long wait has begun.

Chapter 18

Strange," Dany Stevens mumbled to himself. "Very strange," he repeated the sentence and lowered his binoculars.

Dany Stevens was over sixty years old and curious by nature. There was no man of his kind within a few miles of him. He is number one when it comes to curiosity. He wanted to know everything. What his neighbors did, what they bought, with whom and what they talked about. He was a walking encyclopedia of curiosity and knowledge. At least, he thought he was.

When a black limousine arrived, he stood at the window and watched it. He saw two men get out. Both ran up the stairs of Fenton's house. The front door was opened for them. It was spoken, and one man, all military, entered the house. The other stepped back to the car and entered.

Since Dany Stevens was curious, he stooped at the window. He pulled the curtains a little to the side so he could see more. But when a few minutes had passed, he turned his back to the window, walked to the kitchen and fetched chips and beer. Then he sat down on an armchair faced towards the window and watched the scene. However, there was no scene. Everything remained calm. After some time, when the beer can and the pack of chips were empty, he lifted his binoculars. Something was moving inside the house.

The Fenton's front door opened and the family left the house. The driver of the car had opened the car doors. A little later, the car left.

"What's going on?" Dany said. "Is there something wrong?" He shook his head. "Where's Mr. Fenton and the military guy? Neither of them had come out yet. Why do the other family members have bags with them? Why did they leave?"

Questions to which he had no answer. But he wanted answers. He hastily walked to where his telephone was and dialed a number.

Chapter 19

A mobile phone rang across the room. The general looked at his watch. It was 17:32. The Sun outside slowly set itself into the ground. The sky darkens continuously as the light gradually vanishes from sight.

"Yes, Mr. Dumbler?" said the general. General Rock always had a cell phone with him.

"Sir, we're at the airport. The plane leaves in a few minutes. Mrs. Helen Fenton would like to talk to you for a moment."

Mr. Dumbler gave the woman the phone. "Hello, General. How is my husband? Are there any changes?" she asked worriedly.

"He's still lying on the ground, radiating further ahead. Nothing has changed. As soon as I register a movement, I will call you, okay?"

"Thank you," Helen Fenton spoke and returned the handset to Mr. Dumbler. He hung up.

"How's Dad?" Andy asked.

"There's no update yet. We will definitely be contacted by the general as soon as something happens. For now, we must be strong and have faith in both. Everything will be fine."

Mr. Dumbler stopped the limousine. "We are here. The private jet is ready to go. Please disembark and proceed to the plane, everyone."

The family got out of the car and went to the jet. The security guards paved the way for the family, like they're celebrities of some sort. The stern Mr. Dumbler silently walked behind them.

"Where are you taking us?" asked Irina, who hadn't said anything for a long time.

"That information is confidential. However, you will see it soon," she was told, a devastating statement and nothing more.

A little while later, the private jet took off and disappeared between the clouds.

Chapter 20

I hope it's important," the other voice said on the phone.

"As if I never told you anything important," Dany Stevens returned.

"*Dany,*" it came out on the other side. "*What have you got for me? I'm sure you won't just call me for nothing, I assume?*"

The man on the other side was a freelance reporter named Jack Leemann.

"A strange thing had happened. My neighbors left with their luggage."

"*Are you serious? That's why you're calling?! Have you gone crazy with your curiosity? Everybody carries a luggage when they travel. Your age must have been taking a toll on you, my friend.*"

"Knock it! Do you want a story or not? Are you sure you deserve to be called a super journalist?"

"*Yes, of course I do!*"

"Then shut up and let me finish. As I was saying, the family left in a black limousine. I wrote down the number plate. The number is PN 411 107 CY. Let's check it out. I suspect there is more to this than what meets the eye. Something is definitely fishy."

"What makes you so sure?" Jack Leemann asked.

"Because the limousine was driven by a private driver. He took the family with him. But the greatest scoop is yet to come." Dany Stevens made his pause long. He stretched everything to make it even more exciting. "The driver left a man behind. That man is now staying alone with whom I think is the landlord, who is yet to be seen from his window."

"So what? That's just what it was. The two must have talked with each other or something."

"The two definitely had a talk. But what's one of the militaries doing looking for my neighbor with a general's uniform? I can never mistake those four stars on his shoulders."

"Military, huh?" asked Jack Leemann. *"General? That's extraordinary. It's quite strange that the car drove away without a general and leaving a seemingly ordinary person*. A love affair? Are there complications in their marriage?"

"No, they seem absolutely in awe of each other. Disgusting!" Dany Stevens heard nothing more on the other side. "Are you still there?" he asked.

"Yes. I was just thinking. Who's the general with right now? What's his name?"

"He's with my neighbor Mr. Fenton,"

Jack thought and said, "*Erik Fenton? The millionaire?*"

"Yes, what about him?"

"*His name alone is scoop,*" the reporter shouted into the earpiece.

"What have you got, Jack. Is he that important?"

"*I don't know yet, but it could be something. Maybe something big.*"

"You know my address. If it should be of importance, then I expect a cheque from you. Much bigger than the other information before."

"*Such a disgusting thing, Dany. You'd really do everything just for some dirty money. Someday you will be called to account, for your greed and the last for your curiosity.*"

"Let that be my concern. Mind your own business. Keep me informed and don't forget the cheque."

Then Dany Stevens hung up the phone. He moved towards the window front, lifted up his binoculars and looked through. His gaze was fixed on Fenton's house. '*What's going on there?*' was his thought and lowered the binoculars.

Chapter 21

The darkness gave way for a hint of light. It became brighter and Erik Fenton saw himself in a sea of fog. Was it really fog or possibly clouds? He could not identify it.

'It must be cold here,' he thought. But it was neither one nor the other. Erik was only a spirit. He smelled and tasted nothing. He didn't feel any temperature either. He simply walked aimlessly through the fog. He took one cautious step after the other. Again, and again, he whirled up a little fog. Erik felt lost in this infinite sea of fog. *'Is there an end here?'* he asked himself and took a step further. *'Will I finish the steps and will I, as in my dream, meet the guardian?'* He didn't know, so he just kept walking. But suddenly, he hit an object. He looked down and recognized a stone step.

'I am here,' was his thought. Although he didn't need any air to breathe here at this unknown place, he breathed deeply. *'Here, my fate has been decided,'* he thought and wanted to walk up the second stone step when he heard a deep voice behind him.

"Erik...," came out of the fog. Erik Fenton turned around in a hurry and a little frightened. A really long time had passed when he had heard this voice for the last time.

'That voice... I know that voice, don't I?' he thought. The fog lifted and a big giant figure stomped towards him.

Chapter 22

The phone lines at the Department of Defense weren't just hot. They were glowing. Innumerable important information was passed on. In a large room, where the heart of the headquarters was located, it was like a beehive. People ran through this room and brought the latest news to their superiors. On the walls, there were huge screens showing all activities on earth as well as from space. Some employees sat at the computers and looked at the flickering screens. In front of them were the keyboards. With their nimble fingers, they drove over the computer keyboards and passed on information.

A man walked up a staircase from the room and reached a darkened window front. Behind it was a meeting room. Those present could see through the windows what was going on in the central room. The others outside, however, could not see anything behind it. The man reached the glass door with coded forms, opened it and entered. As soon as he had closed the door behind him, he heard no noise from the central room.

"Sorry for the short delay," he said and stepped on a free chair at the meeting table. The other chair was occupied by senior government officials, some generals and military security guards. At the top of the meeting table, a man began to talk.

"What have we got so far?" He had the say in this round,

mostly because he was also the one who informed the President of the United States about the situation. Or so he thought.

"The signals have become stronger," reported the man who had come late. "They are coming from all outside the planet."

"It's not just signals. We have located foreign objects, too. The telescopes are connected with the communication satellites," another reported.

"You mean UFOs," spoke the boss.

"We suspect it is, Sir, and I'm afraid there will certainly be more."

"How...many?"

"Forty, Fifty? Maybe even more."

"So, we are being visited by big UFOs?"

"I think so, Sir. And with the amount of attention, they're giving us, they are certainly not arriving with a peaceful intention."

"Damn," said the boss. "What else do we have?"

"Up to this moment, nothing more except another little thing," a little man at the end of the meeting table reported.

"Yes, please? Who are you?" he was asked.

"My name is James Bloom. Government official and currently the President's personal envoy."

"The President?"

The top man in the table was surprised.

"I'm the one who contacts the President and passes on all the information."

"I don't understand why the President ordered you here. So, what are you doing here?"

"I am here for a message that I am sure will interest you."

"Well, that's something. How important is this communication that we should know about?"

The little man rose from the chair and looked at the other high-ranking men.

"Have you noticed that one man is missing from this group?"

"And who should that be?"

"General Rock," came the answer.

"I don't think General Rock would fit in here. He has nothing to do with interstellar signals from outer space. He's a damn good soldier on the field, but here? I don't understand."

"I wouldn't be so sure. General Rock had a suspicion that has been confirmed. Everyone is on high alert. He was the first to trigger the red alert. That's why he secretly activated all available soldiers worldwide to be prepared in case of a war. He is sure that the earth will be attacked."

The man at the table raised his voice. "He has what?! How dare this man pass us over. He does not have the authority to make such decisions."

"He has actually. A direct authority from the President of the United States. General Rock was also the first to inform the President."

"Well, where is General Rock now?"

"On the road. He seeks help. He tries, in these difficult moments, to get advice from a civilian."

"With a civilian? This becomes more and more of a laughingstock. We are military men. We have everything under control. No mere civilian has the right to interfere with us. If General Rock talks about the military apparatus and gives out secret information, he has behaved disloyally towards us. There will be consequences. The court martial will look forward to him." The man at the table made himself sound important. He started talking about "a civilian," again. "So, who is it?"

"I cannot tell you that. I can only say one thing. I will tell the President about your arrogance."

The high man angrily struck the tabletop with his hand as he stood. "Now that's enough!" he shouted at James Bloom.

"Not yet," Mr. Bloom spoke calmly. "Your job is to activate the communication satellites. In addition, the population should not be informed. We don't want to cause panic and an escape wave on the streets. Everyone should remain calm."

The little man walked to the door and turned around before leaving the meeting room. "One more thing. You say you have everything under control? When it starts and it will start, you will see and realize how much of a failure you are. We just hope General Rock succeeds. Because the civilian, as you say, could be of the greatest importance here."

Then he left the room. It was quiet in the meeting room. No one said anything until the man at the beginning of the table cleared his throat and said, "Well, then. We'll activate the satellites and see what happens. Before you go out again, I want to have the phone number of General Rock's cell phone. Does anyone have it?"

Chapter 23

Erik Fenton now recognized who stood before him. It was Erik, the Viking. His ancestor. That was a surprise! He whispered "Erik...," quietly to himself.

The giant Viking stood in front of Erik Fenton and looked down on him. That was because the Viking was almost two meters higher than him. He looked just like as he used to. On his head, he wore an iron helmet with two horns. Around his wrists, were iron rings and on his waist, the decorated metal belt. The long, dark blond hair came out under the helmet. The beard covered his face. In his hand, he held his mighty axe. As Erik had seen his ancestor for the last time. *'But why is my ancestor here?'* he thought. He had no answer.

"Erik," he whispered to him. "I am surprised to see you!"

"I am not," said the Viking. "I have–no... I had to wait for you for a long time. It's good to see you."

"You waited for me? It's been 25 years since we last saw each other. Why did you wait for me? Does it have to do with the Nameless one?"

"Yes, we are a part of his big plan."

"Plan? I don't understand. What plan?"

"I don't know either. I only know that the Nameless one can anticipate many things in advance. He looks into the future. Even then, when he left us, he knew what would happen next. I am like you, only a small accessory of the big one."

Erik Fenton couldn't do anything with these remarks, but he believed that he would soon learn everything. Perhaps his ancestor knew more than he wanted to admit. Or the Nameless man had made sure that he was not allowed to say anything. Erik was insecure! Why didn't he feel anything although he also carried the Nameless one inside him? It was like a barrier that let him ask further questions.

"Where are we?" he asked the giant. "Why are we here?"

"In the intermediate realm. Near Walhall."

"What?!". On Erik Fenton's forehead, wrinkles and an astonished expression formed in his face. "But why? I don't understand. Shouldn't you already be in Walhall?"

"Yes, but I don't know why I'm still here. The Nameless one certainly knows. All my warriors were allowed inside when they had fallen to dust. I too fell to dust. But as a spirit, I had to run around here and wait for you. I was denied entry. I tried to climb the stairs. The result was tremendous amount of pain and the first time I screamed out my pain. I felt a dark aura seizing me and somehow melting me. Maybe I wasn't worthy enough yet to be accepted into Walhall."

Erik thought and suspected that this was the reason why the face of his ancestor disappeared on the dragon ship.

"At some point, the Nameless one appeared as a ghost in front of me and revealed to me that you were coming. Then, only then, would I perhaps be welcome in Walhall."

"Now I am here and I will help you fulfill your last wish. You will come to Walhall and be reunited with all the brave Vikings."

It sounded like more than just a promise. It was an oath pronounced by Erik Fenton. He believed that the solution could be found in Walhall. The Viking believed the man before him and nodded.

"Is it going in that direction?"

Erik turned to the side.

The Viking said, "Yes," and pointed with his index finger, his raised left hand at the fog in front of him. There were the stone steps.

"I understand. I will walk up the stone steps and face the voice."

"You knew about it," the Viking asked in astonishment.

"I had a dream many months ago that I've been here before. A voice warned me to cross the bridge. Is it the bridge to Walhall? Do you know who it is that guards the entrance?"

"It's the way to Walhall and it's the guardian of the Vikings. Nobody can get past him and certainly not without a weapon."

The Viking raised his right arm. In his right hand, he held an axe.

"Here. Take it with you and go your way."

The giant handed the axe to Erik Fenton. He took it and held it in his right hand. The axe weighed nothing at all. It seemed easy to him.

"Let's see if I can also swing the axe."

He performed two blows through the air. One would not hear the cut through the air. There was no noise.

"You can use them, can you?" asked the Viking.

"Yes. I could. Why do you think I've stayed so fit over the last 25 years? Somehow, I felt that I had to stay active. As much as I could, I practiced secretly with a sword. None of my family knew about it."

"You have a family?"

"Yes. You know my wife when you saved her back then."

"I remember the girl Helen."

"Yes, and we have three children. I hope that I may see them again. But I don't know how everything will end." Erik Fenton had a sad look on his face. Would he see his family again? Then his hand bobbed up and down with the axe. "I will climb the stone stairs and face the guard."

Erik turned around completely and stepped on it. His ancestor only remained armed with a knife. He was proud of Erik Fenton. This man was ready to kill the guard so that the Viking could go to Walhall. Erik Fenton hit the stone stairs with his foot.

'Here goes nothing,' he thought and set one foot after the other. Slowly, he climbed the stone stairs. He didn't know what to expect. Soon, the fog had swallowed him.

Chapter 24

Curiosity and uncertainty gnawed deep into Dany Steven's chest. He walked restlessly through the house and stopped again and again in front of the window. "Damn," he cursed to himself. "Why isn't anything happening?" He was more than tense inside. He already wanted to pick up the binoculars when he cried out. The telephone rang.

Although he knew the shrill tone, this time it seemed louder and more biting to his ears. He hastily picked up the phone. He shouted "Yes," inside.

"It's me Jack," it came out of the other side.

"Jack, damn it. You scared me."

"Tenderly strung?"

"No, just nervous. There was nothing wrong with the house."

"Yes, yes. You and that curiosity of yours."

"Shut up! What do you have to tell me?" Dany Stevens asked, irritated.

"I sneaked myself around for details. Through detours, I came

across secret information. Dany, you have something good. The general used to be a sergeant exactly 25 years ago. He was the one who fought against some aliens in New York."

"How did you figure that out?"

"By the license plate you gave me. Just a few phone calls and I had them. You wouldn't believe who was involved at that time."

"Was it Fenton living across the street from me?" Dany Stevens said.

"Exactly! You're right and you know what I think? I don't think this general just showed up to Mr. Fenton's house for no reason and just to say hello. His family is already gone, as you told me. There must be something in the bush and it must be something mighty."

"But what, don't you know exactly?"

"No, but as soon as I know something, I'll let you know."

"That's too long for me."

"Then do something. Go to the house and look through the windows. Maybe you'll find something. That shouldn't be a problem for you. Nobody will know about it."

"If this general and Mr. Fenton discovers me, it can cost me my collar."

"What's the matter with you? First, you play the curious one

who wants to know and see everything and then you pinch at the simplest task. Move inconspicuously towards the house and if you have discovered something, then call."

Jack Leemann interrupted the line. Dany Stevens slowly let the receiver sink and hung up as well. He was already feeling a bit muddy in his stomach area. *'Should I or I shouldn't?'* were his thoughts. *'If someone catches me, it's over. Then everyone will know about me'.*

Chapter 25

The Vast Outer space. The approaching spacecraft continues to approach Earth with loads of spaceships following its trails. On the cockpit where the leader supervises the journey, there was an amount of tranquility. However, this was bound to change.

"I could locate the signal clearly now," hissed the voice from the control room to the others.

The leader sat on his chair and hissed to himself.

"Let's see how these powerless earthlings get in line when they get a greeting from us."

"How about a laser beam, Sir?" spoke the other being.

"No. Send a black arrow with low scattering power. The coordinates are unambiguous, even if it strikes a few meters before it. My brother will not like this warning but I will."

The leader pushed his stinky breath out. A few seconds later, the ominous projectile shot out of the spaceship into the innocent planet.

Chapter 26

Sir," an employee in the Office of Central Defense called his senior officer. The senior marched towards the man who controlled the screens and configurations of space.

"Yes, what is it?"

"Something is wrong. I went through my program. I am receiving strange data."

"What kind of data do you mean?"

"I'm afraid I don't know what kind. We have these objects flying towards us from all sides. I have located an energy source. It's as if something is cutting through the emptiness of space."

"Can you show me this in more detail on the screen?"

"Just a moment," the man spoke and typed around on the keyboards in lightning speed. Small fields opened up on the screen. It was like a grid. All fields could be analyzed more precisely and enlarged. "The satellites work perfectly," the man said at the computer.

"Here," spoke the official. He pointed to a field in the grid.

"Enlarge this area."

The fingers floated slightly over the keys and the picture was enlarged.

"Now onto the big screen."

A moment later, the screens showed the universe. Everyone present in the room could weakly see what the picture was showing. It was like a black thread coming towards them.

"What could it be?" said the official.

"Sir, it looks like a black arrow. At least that's the way I see it."

"You're right," The officer paused for a moment before continuing. "Can it be that this is the source of energy that you meant?"

"I believe so, Sir."

"Can you tell me where it will hit if it reaches Earth?"

"A moment, please". The man-made hasty movements on the keys and could indicate the exact location a few seconds later. This time the large wall screens indicated a new area. It was Marblehead in Massachusetts. "If the black arrow maintains the direction, it will hit here."

The dot on the map flashed red. It indicated a house on the hill.

"Okay," said the officer. "Who lives there?"

"One moment, Sir."

The sitting man typed the more exact data about the area. The computer worked at full speed and spat out a name. "This house belongs to a Mr. Erik Fenton."

"Fenton...Erik Fenton," the official murmured. "I know that name. I just don't know yet where to locate him."

Chapter 27

The minibus, which was a broadcast van from the local news, slowly drove up the road to Dany Stevens. There were two people in the car with the inscription: "New Live Satellite: Sally Newton and Harry Spikes". They both worked at KW5. Harry drove the car while Sally reads the road map.

"What do you think?" he asked Sally. "Did Jack Leemann just let us drive here for fun? Maybe it's a quack and we did this trip for nothing."

"I don't think so," said Sally. "Jack is very sure about that. If he smells something, then there must be something true or fishy about it."

Sally recently had Jack on the phone. He asked Sally to drive to Dany Steven's house. If something unusual should happen, she had to report to him immediately. Of course, Sally asked why she had to be there. To which Jack just said to watch 'Dany Stevens' outhouse'. That was all.

"We're close. Hit the road up and then turn right," Sally said and put the road map away. Harry Spikes halted the minibus a little away from Dany Stevens house. He turned off the engine and applied the handbrake.

"What now? What's going to happen?" he asked Sally.

"We wait. I don't know what to wait for, but Jack told us to watch the next house."

"Ok," Harry spoke and folded his arms together in front of his chest. "We get paid to work anyway. Whether we do something or not doesn't matter. The main thing is that the money arrives at the end of the month."

"Ugh, what an attitude. Come on, get the camera ready. I'll do the rest."

Harry turned around and left the driver's seat. He moved into the interior of the minibus. He took out his Portable Camera and checked it out. Everything was fine. The battery was charged and the film was inside. Sally handled a technical device beside him.

The whole car was technically equipped. In addition to a mixing console, there was also a cutting machine for the strips and a parabolic antenna on the roof of the minibus. So, one could send direct pictures to the television studio. When both had checked everything, they turned around and looked through the windscreen of the car.

"Someone's inside," Sally said and pointed the right finger at the person.

It was Dany Stevens who just left his house.

"Do you have the camera?"

"Yes," said Harry.

"Then let's go."

The side door of the minibus opened and both persons got out. Sally had a recording device with her. She had it turned on, while Harry carried the camera on her shoulders and captured the pictures. Both of them slowly stepped towards Dany Stevens without him noticing them.

Chapter 28

General Rocks cell phone vibrated. He had set it to silent. There was a reason for that. He didn't want to scare the man lying on the floor with shrill sounds. He didn't know why, but he suspected that this might interrupt something. He said "Yes," quietly. He held the phone by his right ear.

"General Rock," sounded it at the other end.

"Yes. Who is there? How did you get this number?"

"I'm not important. This is NSA Special Agent Ted Gibbs. We had an extraordinary meeting at the Department of Defense a few minutes ago. A Mr. James Bloom was present for you. Mr. Bloom is an emissary of the President and informed us that you were on your way to a civilian for advice? Is that correct?"

"And?"

"The question to you is whether you found this civilian."

"Yes!"

"Could he give you some advice? Possibly one on how we can counter these signals or this alien power."

"I don't know yet. That depends entirely on him."

"Please ask him."

"I can't do that. He left the house for a short time. He will be back soon."

"Aha, I understand!"

"I'll call you back when he comes back and brings you some good advice. Agreed?"

"Alright," Ted Gibbs said and wanted to disconnect.

But something came up. Shortly before, a co-worker brought a report to Ted Gibbs. He skimmed the lines while trying to interrupt the phone call with General Rock.

"A moment, General," he said.

"Yes, please?"

"Where are you right now?"

"As I said. In the house of a civilian."

General Rock did not give away everything so quickly.

"Where is that?" asked Ted Gibbs.

"In Marblehead, Massachusetts. Why?"

"What," screamed the NSA man into the earcup. *"You're where?"*

"In Marblehead!"

"Damn," cursed the man on the other end. *"A few moments ago, we detected a strange energy racing towards us in outer space. The impact will be a house on the hill. The owner is Erik Fenton. Do you know the man?"*

The general said "Yes," surprised and shocked at the same time. To suppress his nervousness, he breathed briefly before handing over a message to Ted Gibbs. "I am in his house."

"Go. Leave the house. We don't know what this may be."

General Rock interrupted the line.
'What am I supposed to do?' he thought and looked at Erik Fenton. He lay on his back and slept in front of him. The bright aura around him was still shining. *'I must not touch him and I do not want to leave him here alone'.* He stood up and took two steps to the left. Suddenly he heard screams and ran to the front door. He opened it and saw who had screamed.

Chapter 29

Dany Stevens curiosity was stronger than reason. A few minutes later he left his house and walked up the street. By this time, the noisy children of the neighborhood were already at home. None of the residents showed up. Dany didn't know yet that curiosity saved his life. He took a few steps towards the Fenton house. Suddenly, it hissed. This hissing became louder and louder. Dany Stevens looked around and then up into the slowly darkening sky. What he saw was incredible. Something came down from the earth's atmosphere. It looked as if a black thread was coming down. The hissing was so loud that Dany Stevens held his ears with his palms. *'What could that be?'* he asked himself and backed away.

His question was answered immediately. The hissing stopped and the black thread disappeared. Dany took the palms off his ears and just stood there. His eyes had followed the flight of this black thing. He now knew where the black thread had struck. Right in his house. What came now was frightening. From the middle the house began to turn black. First the roof, then the outside walls and finally the whole property. Even the green lawn did not remain intact. It turned black. The blackness widened up to the street. Dany Stevens just stood there and felt a vibration under his feet. Although he was in shock, he stepped back. It still vibrated a little, then it stopped. The shock caused Dany, what he saw now, to scream. His house had been black a few seconds ago.

Now it crumbled into black dust. Nothing but a mountain of black dust remained. Even the lawn and the street were not spared. Here, too, a thin layer of dust remained.

He cried out "My house, my house!"

The screams slowly turned into a whimper. He had fallen to his knees and began to cry like a little child.

"Why me, why only me," he whimpered and shook his head.

That he was filmed by Harry and Sally and the neighbors from the houses came he did not notice. He only saw a small light that dazzled him. Then he tilted to the side and fainted.

Chapter 30

Harry Spikes and Sally Newton slowly moved towards Dany Stevens. Harry had set the camera to recording and switched on the small lamp above the lens. The pictures were taken better. Sally had the sound in the camera she was carrying turned on. Both heard the hiss and her gaze wandered towards the sky. Harry held his camera and filmed everything that came in front of the lens. The two of them saw the house in front of them hit by a black thread. The house fell into black dust. "That's a thing," whispered Sally. "I hope you have everything in the box."

"And how! Do you know what that means?"

"Yes. We are the new stars of KW5."

He kept filming and panning his camera around. He captured not only Dany Stevens, who was sitting on the floor whimpering and distraught, but also the house, which is why both had come from the transmitter.

At Erik Fenton's front door stood a man in uniform. He had watched everything and moved back inside. The front door was closed. For Harry, that didn't matter anyway. With the zoom in feature of the camera, he had pulled the man so close to himself that you could see his face. Then he interrupted the shot and let the camera slide down. He also turned off the light.

"What do you mean Sally? Are we cutting this tape back together and sending it through the channel?"

"Yes. Go to the bus. I'm going to clean up a bit. This is going to be a big deal."

The two of them turned around and walked back to the outside broadcast van. They didn't see that Dany Stevens tilted to the side and remained motionless.

Chapter 31

General Rock stood at the front door and saw a man standing on the street. He kept screaming "My house! My house!" But what surprised him the most was why the man screamed so loudly. The house further down was no more. Only black dust.

'So, this is where the alien energy hit. It didn't hit us. What bad luck,' he thought.

The neighbors came out of the other houses to see who was screaming. Further down General Rock discovered two people. He quickly realized that these two were not from here. He turned around and disappeared back inside the house. He quickly pulled out the cell phone and pressed a number. It was the one from the Department of Defense. Immediately he got someone on the phone.

"This is General Rock. I'd like to speak to NSA Special Agent Ted Gibbs, please."

"Just a moment, please."

The line clicked and he had the man on the other end.

"The shot missed," said General Rock.

"We saw it through the spy satellites. Somehow this shot was diverted. You're lucky that the strange energy hit the house next door."

"Yes, I can say that. Listen to me Mr. Gibbs. I just saw two suspicious people on the street. They could be TV reporters. I suspect they recorded everything. For the sake of national security, I would be in favor of you sealing off the entire area from the military. Also, the air sector must not be penetrated. If someone from the other transmitters gets wind of it, then it is over with calm. Seal everything off as best you can and cut off the telephone lines. But what I can use here is an ambulance. I'm sure the man on the street needs help. I'll get back to you as soon as Mr. Fenton is back."

Then, he broke the connection and stepped back to the couch. Outside it got darker as the sun disappeared behind the horizon. General Rock turned on the floor lamp in the corner, sat down on the couch and looked at the man lying on the floor. It hasn't changed.

'What am I supposed to do when there's another attack?' the general thought. He didn't know. The long wait had already begun a long time ago.

Chapter 32

The stone stairs never seemed to stop. Erik suddenly heard a noise. 'Why can I hear something here and not at the bottom?' he asked himself and walked further up. The fog lifted a little and he saw an object he had seen before in his dream. It was elongated and stood next to the stone stairs. Erik came closer to the object and recognized what it was. It was a dark, partly wet wooden post. There were strange things hanging from it. Erik's eyes were wide open. He shook with horror. At the wooden post fibrous threads and small ropes hung down. On these hung axes, swords, knives, a shield and heads. Skulls!

Also on the ground, around the post, lay some of these pale skulls around. At the end of the post a skull looked down. Black were the eye sockets and the nose. The lower jaw was missing. On the bare skull was an old Viking helmet. This wooden post looked terrible.

'*What is that?*' Erik thought. '*Is that a totem or a trophy post?*' Disgusted, he looked away. '*Will I lie here soon?*' was his thought. He did not come further to think. A thundering voice let his blood freeze in his veins.

"Every mortal who dares to cross the bridge must die. I am the guardian. Come closer and face death."

Erik had heard this sentence months ago. He grasped his axe hard. He raised his right hand slowly and looked in the direction where the voice came from. Soon he saw a shadow approaching him and saw the guard. *'What a colossus'* he thought. *'I can't get past him!'*

The Guardian was a Viking and what a valant Viking. He wore almost the same clothes as Erik's ancestor. But the upper body was more muscular than anything that had ever been there. In addition, this Viking was one head taller than Erik, the Viking. Calculated in masses, over two meters thirty. But what frightened Erik Fenton was not only his height, but the huge axe in the Viking's hands. The axe was razor-sharp and had a longer wooden handle as an extension. With this axe the Viking could keep the enemies at a distance. So, he could kill them from far away. Erik had practiced for years. Today he wanted to know and he had good chances. The Viking had to swing the axe. This allowed Erik to dive under the axe and approach the guard. He had imagined that. Whether it also worked would show itself. But before he spoke to the guard.

"I am Erik Fenton. My ancestor, Erik, the Viking, is waiting for a sign at the beginning of the stone steps. A sign, so that he may come to Walhall. I am here to pave his way."

The Viking in front of Erik looked down on him and began to laugh. "You wight. No one has ever passed me. No one has ever defeated me. Nobody! You will die like everyone else and become my trophy. You have courage, mortal. I must admit this. That is why I will put your head on the wooden post."

"There already is one. You don't have room for a second one.

Come here and show what you can do."

Chapter 33

Space. "The coordinates were accurate. The projectile reached the target and a little lost, as intended, it hit a dwelling next door," the creature reported from the control room.

"Good," the leader hissed at the other.

He made hissing and growling noises.

"We will continue to approach the earth. Say it to the others as well. Today we will leave the people alone. Tomorrow, when the sun rises in this area, everything will decide."

"There is still something," said the other being in the control room.

"What," hissed the leader.

"I receive signals from outside. People have a kind of machine in the outer atmosphere. These have been activated."

"What machines! Dangerous weapon systems?"

"The speech and word converter is currently determining it. Yes, now I see it. No, these metal machines are used for communication. There are almost seven hundred of this kind in orbit. Also, a larger amount of metallic garbage. That's how the sensors indicate it."

"What do people want with these things? Negotiate and beg for mercy?"

"Maybe. Or they capitulate before we arrive on Earth. That would be an advantage. We might well need them for slavery on the other planet."

"A good idea," said the leader. "But we don't need many of them. The rest will be destroyed tomorrow."

Chapter 34

Erik Fenton risked a big lip. He wanted to provoke the guard. This Viking was so taken with his ego that he might have made mistakes. These words from a mortal did not please the Sentinel. He looked closely at the man in front of him. Then he lifted his axe and the sharp leaf swung towards Erik's body. Erik ducked as the sharp axe cut across him. He could still hear the whistling of the blade above his head. Then he lifted his body and took one step, then another towards the guard. He held the axe of his ancestor firmly in his right hand. Now he was very close to the Viking. Erik lifted the axe over his right shoulder and struck. But the Viking knew how to help himself. He quickly turned in the direction where Erik stood. The hard handle of the mighty axe slowed down Erik's blow. The Viking held his hard hands to the end of the handle and below the axe. The giant thought that this would be enough to stop the mortal. But he realized that Erik had done something no one had done before. Erik's blow was so hard that the back of the axe handle broke.

Astonishment was written in the eyes of the guardian. But he didn't want to give up. The left hand threw away the useless piece of wood. With his right hand he held the shortened axe in his hands and struck at lightning speed. Erik could only save himself with one step back. But the axe found its way to Erik. He was hit on his left upper arm. The axe continued to run and hit his upper body. Erik felt a pain that made him groan. At first, he was confused. He only existed as a spirit in this intermediate world. Or did he not? Was everything reality? And yet he felt the pain.

'Am I going crazy?' he thought. *'Why do I feel my body?'*

He looked down at himself briefly and discovered how his shirt turned red through the cut. Fortunately, these were only cuts. He had little time to act. He wanted a decision and quickly. The Viking was still in his element. Due to the blow, he was in such a rage that he underestimated his opponent. Erik threw himself forward and came even closer to the Viking than before. He clashed with him and held the axe under the giant's throat.

He said "It's over," to the guard. "Let me pass and you will live."

The Viking was so surprised by Erik's appearing that he only looked at him with big eyes. He felt the cold sharp axe at his throat. He rolled his eyes and nodded slowly. After all, he didn't want to die. Erik believed him and took the axe from his throat. Then he took a step back. He had to be careful because the stone steps were still damp from the fog. A wrong kick and Erik would fall into nowhere. The guard stood straight and looked at the man in front of him.

"Who are you?" he asked.

"I already told you that. I am Erik Fenton. Descendant of Erik, the Viking."

"Mortal. You defeated me. With cunning and strength. I give you the way to Walhall!"

The guard made way and Erik walked past the giants. He didn't see the short grin in the guard's face. After a few stone steps the fog was again so thick that he could not see any stone steps. Slowly he felt his way upwards. One wrong step and he was gone. Suddenly the fog lifted and he saw bright light in this dimension, as he called it. It came down from above and brightened the surroundings even more. Erik saw the stone staircase, which made a curved arch. It was a kind of bridge he saw. But what fascinated him the most was the end of the bridge. There stood a mighty castle.

Erik whispered "Walhall," and walked over the stone bridge towards his destination.

Chapter 35

General Rock was sitting on the couch. After a long wait, he stood up and moved to the left side. He didn't suspect anything evil. That's why the sound just heard came as a surprise. It was a groan. He whirled around and looked at Erik Fenton. He was the one who made the noise. The general stepped back and looked at the man. He didn't like what he saw. On his left upper arm, he discovered a narrow red thread. It was a cut. Slowly the shirt fabric absorbed the blood and became wider.

'What do I do?' the general thought. *I may not touch him'*. His eyes became even bigger now. The chest was cut again. The shirt absorbed the blood here as well. *'What happens here. What happens to him? Is he in a truth dream?'*. The general could not help him and was doomed to watch.

Chapter 36

Sally Newton was ready. She had tied her hair back and done herself a bit of good. Her lips were shining red. "Are you ready?" she asked Harry Spikes.

"Yes!"

"Adjust everything and then get out." Harry pressed some buttons and immediately had connection with the transmitter.

"What is," he was asked by the line.

"We have a sensation. Put us in the special news."

"Are you crazy? You can't be serious. They are already full."

"But not from what we recorded earlier."

"I just hope it's good, otherwise you'll lose your jobs."

"No fear. We keep our job. In addition, there is also a fat danger bonus with wage increase."

"We'll talk about this later," the station's director in charge said.

"When will you be ready?"

"In exactly ten seconds."

"Okay. Then show what you have," said the director, who was also the director.

Harry nodded to Sally, who was standing in front of the outside broadcast van. She had put on a lady's jacket and a skirt. The microphone in her right hand. In the background some houses. Harry had the camera on his shoulders. He could now transmit everything directly. "Three, two, one and...," he gave the starting signal.

At that moment, station KW5 was broadcasting the latest news to households. "Good evening. This is Sally Newton from TV channel KW5. Tonight, I witnessed an extraordinary spectacle. Here in Marblehead a tragic incident happened. I dazzle them with this incident." Harry pressed a button on the control panel and the pictures were sent with comment. Everyone in this area and even further away could follow the spectacle. Then the picture disappeared and Sally reappeared on the air.

"You've seen it, ladies and gentlemen. What I showed them here was not an illusion. That was real! I wonder if this black thread was not an attack from space. Are there other black threads coming down trying to destroy us? If so, who wants to harm us? Who could be interested in us? Maybe on the man wearing a military uniform? Was the attack with him? Tonight, I could see him."

Harry pressed the button again. Everyone saw General Rock

standing at the front door. Then he disappeared inside. The show went straight again. Sally had received all the information from Jack Leemann before the show. That's why she was so well prepared.

"This man is General Rock. He used to be a sergeant and was involved with aliens 25 years ago. Is today another day when the aliens come back? Who can know that? Not us, but the military! What is the President of this nation not telling us? I will keep you informed. For KW5 from Marblehead, Sally Newton."

The broadcast was interrupted. Harry turned the camera off and put it aside.

"That was great," he said. "We came out big."

"Yes. That's us."

Now they heard and saw an ambulance coming at them. The car shot up the road and stopped at Dany Stevens' destroyed house.

"Quick the camera," called Sally.

You didn't have to tell Harry that twice. He turned it on while he was lifting it and filmed it.

"What's going on with you," shouted a voice from the outside broadcast van?

"Shit," cursed Harry. "Him again."
It was the director boss.

"Not now," Harry spoke and turned off the switch.

Both saw the ambulance stop and the paramedics jump out. They ran towards the man lying on the floor and examined him. Then one of them fetched the stretcher and loaded the man onto it. Within a few minutes it was all over. The ambulance rushed away.

The two of them wanted to get into the car when they heard a thunder. It was as if a thousand elephants were walking through the streets. The ground vibrated strongly. Harry panned the camera around and saw a heavy metal vehicle. It was an armored car rolling up the road. The two heard a voice from inside the armored car.

"Put the camera down and step back. That's an order."

"Hey, we're not military henchmen that you can command around."

"You will do it!"

"If not," Sally shouted after the voice.

"Then we open fire."

"You can't do that. We live in a free country. Everybody may represent his opinion."

"Not today," spoke the voice.

The armored car turned a little and the fire tube swiveled to the outside broadcast van.

"Curse it! Let's get away from here. They're serious," Sally said and ran to the side like Harry.

There was a loud bang and the armored car had fired its grenade. The broadcast van exploded and a jet of flame shot up. The surroundings were brightly lit. The people in the houses were frightened when they heard the bang and began to pray. No one dared to go outside. Everyone knew or could guess what had happened tonight. Everyone had seen the news on television. So, it was true! It was an attack from outer space. That was the confirmation, because otherwise the military would not be here. What in a few minutes, after large parts of the nation had seen the contribution, began hell? The chaos was perfect!

That was what the Department of Defense, General Rock and the President of the United States wanted to avoid. It was too late now.

Chapter 37

The Ministry of Defense was in an even more hectic situation. NSA Special Agent Ted Gibbs was raging. Everyone had arrived in the meeting room and listened to the words of the NSA man.

"Curse it!" screamed Ted Gibbs. "I spoke to the President. There is a national state of emergency. Everything is made tight. What he will soon announce through the National Television of the Nation is his task. But I have another task. It's more of a problem.

I want to know why someone from the television station KW5 was there where the black arrow was struck. Someone must have informed them. Check the phone lines from the area and the station. I want to know everything. Who's behind it – everything. Do you understand me?"

The others were intimidated. They jumped up and left the meeting room. Other employees stayed there.

"It's a national emergency," he continued. "Everything is closed down. You will ensure that this will be so until new orders come. The Luftwaffe will fly continuously and nobody should come and tell me he needs to be off duty. This is about saving our nation. Perhaps also around the earth. So, move your asses."

The rest of the men left the meeting room in a hurry. Ted Gibbs was alone. He had calmed down again, although he was still agitated inside. His thought was with General Rock and maybe this Erik Fenton had some advice. He could only hope.

Chapter 38

Erik walked over the stone bridge. The bright light above him was like a signpost. In between he looked down. One wrong step and he would fall into infinity.

'What is down there?' he thought. 'Is there Niflhel, the realm of the dead? Or are there the Ungudds. The evil spirits which the Vikings call them?'

Erik had already read countless books about the Nordic peoples. He knew a lot more than other people. After all, he was already in another time himself and had swung the sword with the Vikings. The end of the bridge came and he felt strange.

'I am in Walhall. The home of the Viking Gods' he thought. 'But how is such a thing possible?'

He shook his head to clear his mind. Because he wanted to concentrate on the upcoming one. Erik walked across a large square and a few steps separated him from the walls of Walhall. It was not only the walls he saw from afar, but also the huge wooden gate. Stone statues of Vikings stood on both sides. They were as high as the door. They were a kind of guardian. Erik approached the wooden gate. Nobody seemed to be here. He looked to both sides. No one showed up.

'*The only thing is, I open the gate and enter. Or I'll knock first*' he thought jokingly. The gate was massive. '*Here you certainly have to use your strength to open it*'. He put the axe to the ground and pressed his palms against the wooden gate. As much as he pressed against it, the gate could not be opened. '*What am I doing? The gate is too heavy and to smash this gate with the axe does not have to be. I would need an eternity until I am through! There must be another way!*'

He took a closer look at the wooden gate and discovered something on the right side of the gate. It was a metal ring. '*Aha, this must be some kind of doorbell here*' he thought. He grasped the metal ring, which was heavy, and lifted it up. Then he dropped it back. The metal ring banged against the wooden gate and a metallic sound was created. Erik even heard a reverberation from the inside out here. '*It must be a big hall behind it*'.

A few moments passed and he heard a grinding noise. The gate gave way. As if by magic, the wooden gate opened and opened the entrance. Erik took a deep breath and crossed the threshold. The darkness was there. No light, no sign. No one was there and yet someone had to be there, otherwise the gate would never have opened. He stood a few steps away from the gate wing. He held the axe firmly in his right hand. The gate closed behind him with a dull bang. Erik stood in the darkness waiting for a sign.

Chapter 39

Good evening, ladies and gentlemen. The President of the United States." So, the spokesman announced the entrance into the hall of the highest man of the country.

The room was bursting with reporters. The cameras were already running. The door opened and the President entered. He stepped towards the podium with a serious expression and paused for a moment. In his face, countless unspoken thoughts were written. He wanted to express some of them tonight.

He spoke "Good evening," into the microphone.

It was not only a greeting for those present in the hall, but also for the rest of the nation. Every possible television station was present and transmitted this moment.

"You've all seen," the President began "this terrible event at Marblehead. Many wonders if this was not a deception. This is not so. We were hit by an alien source of energy on Earth. This energy was fired from an unknown object in space, and we have no contact yet. I am a man who wants and wants to protect the nation. That was always my goal. Tonight, I will make my decision. For me this is a declaration of war on our nation and the rest of the world. All governments have been informed. The preparations for a possible war are in full swing. Whether we will succeed in averting a war will be seen in the coming hours. I am against war and that is why the Ministry of Defense is working on a solution at all levels.

In the meantime, I ask all citizens of our country to keep a cool head and behave in a disciplined manner. Stay in your homes. It is no use if you leave everything in your head to escape. We wouldn't get far because we don't know if and where another energy will hit us. Don't go out on the streets. These should be empty so that the National Guards can secure them. Only the military and authorized persons are allowed to move on them. The state of emergency has now come into force. Individual criminals and organized gangs who plunder the shops and are caught are executed without trial on the spot. No matter man, woman or youth. Thank you."

The President turned away and left the room to the indignation of the journalists present. They wanted to ask a few more questions, but the President had already slipped through the door.

Chapter 40

Half an hour later. General Rock's cell phone hummed. "Yes." He held the phone by his right ear and spoke softly into it.

"This is Mr. Dumbler, Sir?"

"Yes, Mr. Dumbler?"

"We have arrived. The family wants a report on Mr. Fenton's condition."

"He is still shrouded in this bright light. Nothing has changed."

He now had to make a white lie. He was not allowed to say anything about the wounds on Erik's body.

"Sir? Did you see the news on the station?"

"Yes. I've been turning on the TV for a long time and turning it as quietly as possible."

"We passed one of the rooms when the TV was on. The family saw everything. They are holding on bravely. That's what I wanted to tell you, Sir."

"Thank you, Mr. Dumbler. My thoughts are with the family.

Should something happen here, I'll call. Don't worry."

Then he broke the connection. Again, he was alone with the mute and injured man.

Chapter 41

Suddenly Erik heard a voice from the darkness. He was almost frightened by that voice. "Mortal. Step closer."

"Where should I go? It is dark and I see no way."

Erik was already right about that. There could be an abyss everywhere. A wrong step and he had been Erik Fenton.

"Is there a mortal fear of darkness?" he was asked.

What was he to do? He did not believe that the power of the Nameless man would let him come this far and then do something to him.

"No! Not before darkness. Only discomfort before the unknown. I will come. Where are you?" Erik said into the darkness.

"Go straight out, then up the stone steps. Above I will receive you," spoke the voice.

Erik did as he was told. Carefully and one step at a time he set off. Then he hit something hard. It was the stone steps. The higher he walked up these, the more the darkness thinned out. Above, at the end of the stone steps, it was bright. Something flickered irregularly. *'Those must be torches. But where does the wind that moves them come from?'* Erik arrived at the top step and was overwhelmed by what he saw.

Chapter 42

Despite the President's call to stay at home, thousands of people fled by car from the cities. Escape was only a word with great effect. Cars crashed into each other. People were injured. The hospitals were overcrowded with injured people. The doctors worked at the limit of their strength with full commitment. The streets were dirty. Everywhere there was dirt from newspaper papers, rubbish bins and even parts of the furnishings. So, the waste could also be disposed of. It didn't belong to anyone. Besides the dirt piles on the streets, the National Guard was in action. Jeeps with machine guns were brought into position as well as armored cars. In all cities of the nation and in the whole world there was this escape. The chaos was perfect.

Chapter 43

The President walked through the corridors with his confidants. "What else does the Ministry of Defense have in store for us," he asked an employee.

"So far nothing new, Mr. President!"

"Where's the Secretary of Defense? I expect his report, what he has done so far."

"He's stuck at the airfield. He drove there by car and got into the traffic jam as expected. He will take the military helicopter and get here as soon as possible."

"What have we got from Ted Gibbs and James Bloom?"

"Nothing yet, Sir. I am sure, however, as soon as they have something, they will call us immediately."

"Have they found out who tipped off the private station?"

"Yes, Sir. We were able to arrest the two reporters. The same goes for the man who tipped them off. It's a Mr. Jack Leemann. He got the information from someone else. A man named Mr. Dany Stevens. He was "erased," from the house with the alien energy."

"So, we owe it all to Dany Stevens."

"Yes, Sir. He's considered very curious in the neighborhood. He watched a Mr. Erik Fenton's house and saw General Rock arrive. We learned that from Ted Gibbs in the meantime."

"Where is he now?"

"At the clinic. He suffered a seizure because of the loss of his house."

"When he recovers, we will bring him to justice."

The men walked through the corridors and disappeared behind a door.

Chapter 44

The senior supervisor was called once again. "Sir," said a Defense Department employee.

He said "Yes," and walked towards the man.

"Do you want to take a look, Sir?" The employee pointed to the monitor. "The data confirms it. The surveillance satellites now have a better image resolution."

"On the main screen."

The man at the control panel pressed a button and the big screens on the wall showed the universe. Suddenly there was silence in the room. What the present got to see was unique. Everyone could recognize the different floating objects. These did not look peaceful. They were utopian spaceship shapes with many spines on the sides and on others hanging indefinable things.

"My God," someone whispered behind the men.

Without turning around everyone knew who it was. It was NSA Special Agent Ted Gibbs. He saw everything and his face darkened.

"The UFOs left the moon behind and stopped in front of the

orbit," said the man at the switchboard.

"I can see that myself," said Ted Gibbs. "As if they were waiting for something."

"A sign," spoke another employee. "Maybe they're waiting for a message from us?"

"That is possible. Or to attack us at the right time. In any case, the weapon systems on the communication satellites are switched on. First, we send you our best welcome greetings. If they really want to harm us, as they have already done, then we will not surrender without a fight."

Chapter 45

A mysterious voice hissed out of the dark room, "Tell everyone to stop their ships. We are already very close. I'm sure the planet's inhabitants have already recognized us."

"We wait until the sun rises on our side. Then we attack. Only where my treacherous brother hides, no fire may be opened. Tell the others."

The message was sent and the enemy spaceships waited for the moment of attack.

Chapter 46

Erik looked into the big hall. From right to left burning torches were stuck in the wall brackets. The hall was well lit. In front of him, in the middle, stood a Viking statue. Below it was a stone throne. On the sides of this throne lay countless signs and dozens of skulls distributed on the ground. Pale and with empty eye sockets they lay there and it seemed as if every skull would fix Erik. Next to the stone throne stood a large axe and a sword.

What almost took Erik's breath away were the people standing in the hall. On the stone throne sat a Viking giant. On his head he wore a helmet with horns. The white hair hung down under the helmet in long strands. He also wore a white long beard. The arm muscles tightened hard and the metal rings shone around the muscles. Next to the throne stood a great Viking. He held a heavy powerful hammer in his right hand. He was dressed more plainly than the other Vikings standing gathered in the hall. Erik counted over ten Vikings without the one sitting on the stone throne. Through the many illustrations in the history books of Norwegian legends, he could imagine who was sitting in front of him. Before he could only think the thought or whisper in front of him, the person sitting spoke to him.

"Step closer, mortals. We have waited for you."

Awed that Erik could experience this moment in his life, bowed before the Viking. The giant stood up and took a step forward.

"Odin," whispered Erik.

"Yes, it is me. That is my name."

His voice really sounded like a deity, echoing and commanding with power.

"The God of the Vikings," Erik whispered to himself again.

"Yes, and do you know who the others are?" he was asked.

"No."

"These are all my brave Vikings who have been loyal to me for ages. You should know the Viking on my right side. It is my bravest warrior. My son Thor."

"Thor," Erik quietly pronounced the name.

'The hammer...the hammer is the Mjöllnir. That's how it is called. When the Viking hits it, no grass grows anymore,' Erik thought.

"I can see from your face that you have questions."

"Yes, I do," said Erik.

"Then ask, mortal! You...are the last of the ancestral line."

"Why did you expect me? Why am I here? Why do you know

that I am the last of the ancestral line? Why was my ancestor, whose axe I carry with me, not allowed to go to Walhall? Why was it denied him? That is all I want to know at the moment."

He waited for an answer and looked the god of the Vikings in the eye. Somehow, they were glassy. Yes, almost transparent.

"I see you have the courage to look into my eyes. Trying to penetrate them. You will not succeed. No blood flows in my veins and I have no skin. I am only a spirit and nevertheless, my body is impenetrable." He hit his chest with his fist.

Erik found everything uncanny and understood nothing. He hoped that the Viking would enlighten him.

"Do mortals always ask so many questions at once even though they already know some of the answers?"

"I don't understand... ."

"Well, I'll answer it for you." The deity took another step towards Erik. He wanted to face him. "Do not try to deceive me, mortals. Don't you dare attack me. That wouldn't get you anywhere good. Am I right, Guardian?" Odin spoke past Erik.

Behind Erik, the guard had sneaked quietly from the stone bridge. He stood half a meter behind Erik. He had lifted the axe halfway up. Erik Fenton slowly turned around and saw the muscle mountain in front of him.

"I'm not going to fight you again, guard. I already defeated you earlier."

"That was no victory," he said. "I wanted you to show me how you humans fight on earth. Whether there are still true warriors or not. I let you win. You were brave. That is why I let you go on."

Erik still did not understand. Why he was here. He turned around and looked at Odin.

"Are you ready to experience everything. mortal?"

Erik nodded.

"Then, listen to every word I say."

Chapter 47

A voice hissed in the dark, "I'm receiving some data here."

"What is it?"

"The language converter is working on it. Now I see it. The planet inhabitants are sending us a message. It is a welcome greeting."

"They choose to welcome us? Even after we have sent them a greeting? Yes, I like that. Send them one, too. But, when the sun rises on the side, we will send other kind of greetings."

The leader made hissing noises.

Chapter 14

Ages ago where the time in Walhall has no meaning, me and my warriors felt a strange aura. It was a force that stepped over the stone bridge to our wooden door. Without opening, it penetrated through the wooden gate, broke through the darkness like a light sword and entered the hall. My warriors jumped up and stood in front of me armed, ready to fight on whatever what or who would dare attack. Not that we were afraid, but a malaise crept up on our legs. However, it quickly evaporated when the aura spoke to us.

"What did this aura look like?" asked Erik.

"It was a big figure. Bright, like a thousand shining suns. I could not see the face. In any case, it was an unknown being. Then it introduced itself. The voice was soft and it radiated trust. The aura or the being was called, "the Nameless."

'The Nameless,' thought Erik. *'He had appeared here in Walhall. But why had he come?'*

Odin continued. "The Nameless one had crossed the boundaries of the dimensions by his power, so he called them, and made it this far into the realm of the Vikings. It wanted to apologize to us, to me, because it misused the last Vikings for its own purposes. My warriors took down their weapons. I accepted the apology and continued to listen to the being. The Nameless one knew everything about Walhall and us. It also knew the future which he let us know, too. Now we understood why we could not go any further."

"I don't understand you," said Erik Fenton. "Where to go?"

"We... me, the warriors in Walhall could not just go. We had to wait for eternity until all the Vikings here were allowed to come to Walhall, to their homeland. Only if everyone were here would we melt into a single entity. Then we would be immersed in the next, Divine Spheres. We were Vikings, gods in the past, where there were only warriors. Only a few of your people would still remember us. We have fallen into oblivion and become meaningless."

Erik Fenton understood. The gods needed the last of the Vikings to cross over into their next life.

"Then you're missing Erik the Viking, my ancestor to become a perfect part."

"Yes, for Erik, the Viking, we have waited an eternity. But he did not come. All the other brave Vikings are already in Walhall."

"But why didn't he come? He was eagerly waiting for the entrance to Walhall! He would only have to walk up the stone steps."

"It's not that simple. All the Vikings who died on the Drakkar crumbled to dust and arrived here. Except Erik. When he wanted to climb the stone steps, he felt immense pain. And he felt it so violently that he almost died of it, although he is only a ghost. If this had not happened, then we would not get any further. We would be damned to stay here for all eternity."

Erik Fenton's thoughts overturned. A suspicion aroused in him, which he held almost impossible. Or not at all? Should he ever come back, he wanted to bring him to justice. But was it really necessary to do this? Was it perhaps one of the plans of the Nameless man why his ancestor had to stay?

"Did the Nameless man promise you anything?" asked Erik.

"Only that he still wanted Erik, the Viking, and us too. But we don't know why."

"But I do. My thoughts have gone on wanderings and added up one and one. I believe that something more will come to you. If it is so far, I cannot say. The Nameless one will definitely contact you. I will go now and visit my ancestor."

"Wait," Odin said. "I still have something for you."

He nodded to one of his warriors. He turned around, grabbed something and handed Odin a small box. Odin took it and gave it to Erik Fenton.

"What is that?" he asked curiously.

"Look inside."

Slowly, he opened the small box. During the opening, a bright light penetrated from the inside of the box. Erik had now opened it completely and looked into the light.

"Looks like a tablet," he said.

In fact, the light came from a round object. It really looked like a tablet.

"What do I do with it?"

"The Nameless one will have thought something of it when he left her with me. She is meant for you. He also said that you must take her and thus experience everything. But do not underestimate this little thing. It is a part of his power. Use it well," Odin said. Erik reached into the box and grabbed the round thing. As soon as he had touched it the light went out and he held the tablet between his fingers.

He knew exactly that he could trust the Nameless one. Without hesitation he took it in his mouth and swallowed it down. It was as if he started to burn. From the inside out. That calmed down. After a few moments it was all over. Erik wanted to turn away and leave the gods, but Odin held him back.

"If you see Erik, the Viking, tell him we are waiting for him!"

"I will. Farewell, gods!"

Chapter 49

Ministry of Defense. "S.E.T.I. sent us a message," the man at the control panel said. This information was for the superior.

"What did she say?" he asked.

"The UFOs have reported. It seems as if they got our message. A message was also sent to us in our language. They apologize for the mistake they made. There was no intention to shoot the black arrow."

The superior just made "hmm...," and thought.

"I don't believe them. We continue."

Ted Gibbs, who stood behind both of them, said "That's my opinion too. All weapons are at our disposal. Except nuclear weapons. If there is an attack, we will shoot back."

Then Ted Gibbs left the two.

Chapter 50

Erik Fenton left Walhall. He walked unerringly through the darkness of the hall. The wooden gate opened and he saw the bright light above him. After a few steps, he reached the stone bridge. Worrying thoughts flooded his brain. Among other things, he now knew why the Nameless being had been here in Walhall. He needed reinforcements, who'll take up the fight against strangers. Hurriedly, and yet with every step-in mind, he hurried over the stone bridge, then went down. A little later in the fog, he suddenly saw the wooden post. *'It's not that far anymore,'* he thought.

And it was. He reached the end of the stone steps and looked around. Erik, the Viking, was not there. Erik called for him and moments later, the giant came out of the fog towards him.

"Here," Erik spoke to his ancestors and presented them with the borrowed axe. "It served me very well."

"Were you in Walhall?" asked the Viking.

"Yes. It is wonderful. I met Odin, Thor and the other Vikings."

"You met them all?"

"I talked to them. It was an honor for me."

"What did they say? Did they say why I was not allowed to go to Walhall?"

"They did not know. But I suspect that you still have to have a little patience. When the time has come, they will certainly come for you. Meanwhile, I–!"

Erik suddenly got tired, as if all his energy had left him. He couldn't talk any further. Then a darkness came towards him, which made him tilt forward. He did not even notice that he fell towards the ground and remained lying, motionless. Even his ancestor was surprised by this incident. He wanted to help and hold the man before falling. It failed. As soon as Erik Fenton lay on the ground, something unusual happened. His body dissolved and disappeared before the Viking's eyes.

Chapter 51

Erik's eyes fluttered open and he saw a black sky. But looking closely, he realized it wasn't the sky. It was space. Above, beside and below him, he saw thousands of stars shining propitiously. Further down he saw the earth, the earth's atmosphere and he floated there. He felt free and light like a feather. It was a breathtaking view and an emotional moment. But that moment did not last long. His gaze darkened when he saw the countless alien spaceships in space. *'They are here'* he thought. *'They have come to harm and destroy the earth. I must warn the others.* That was just a thought. Then he saw himself floating towards the earth. He came closer and closer and he broke through the earth's atmosphere. Suddenly it was dark again around him. But the darkness did not last long. The creature from the alien spaceship hissed something out. "I feel its aura. He is nearby. I hate him and all who help him," he hissed hatefully.

Chapter 52

General Rock had walked back and forth in the living room for a long time. Again, and again, he'd look at the lifeless body of Erik Fenton. Suddenly, it seemed as if the glow was fading. He approached the man and looked at him. *'The glowing stopped,' he* thought.

A short time later, it had disappeared. Erik Fenton opened his eyes. He squinted his eyes a little. Even when it was night outside, a light dazzled him. He recognized what it was. The floor lamp in the corner of his living room dazzled him. It wasn't the only thing he saw. A face hovered over him. General Rock bent over and looked at him.

"Are you all right, Mr. Fenton?" he asked quietly.

He was not prepared for the reaction of the man lying on the ground. Erik's left arm shot up and his hand squeezed the general's neck. He began to gasp for air and tried to loosen the hard strangling.

"I'm fine," said Erik, "and what I want from you are not only answers, but also the truth, understand?"

"I... I–," the general ruffled.

Erik loosened the stranglehold and let go of the general's neck. Then he straightened up. The general retreated and grabbed his own neck. He turned around and went to the salon table. There was the water glass. He hastily dumped the cool water into his throat. He coughed and spit water out.

He cursed, "damn it!" with a sigh. "What was that about?"

Erik Fenton stood up and took the water bottle. He drank it in one gulp. It did him good. As soon as he had taken it from his lips, he put it back on the table. He looked at the general.

"I'm waiting," he said.

"For what? I don't know what you're talking about," said the general who had found the language again. "You almost crushed my larynx."

He rubbed his neck.

"It's about my ancestor. Erik, the Viking."

"What about him? I don't know anything. However, I'll be glad to help you find things out. What happened when you went on the Drakkar? –". The general felt queasy in his stomach. It clicked in his head, "Now I know what you mean."

"So., I wait?"

"Like I said, we were on our way to the Drakkar. When some of my crew and I jumped the tide and swam to the ship, the helicopter was above us. As soon as I jumped on board, I felt strange. I felt as if I had to do something. Suddenly, a strange force penetrated my head and gave me the order. The helicopter rotated above us and whirled everything up. I saw countless small piles of dust on the deck before they were blown away. Only a single pile of dust remained and it lit up a little. The glow was the same as I had seen before. I passed the message to the helicopter. I needed a vessel that would allow me to capture the dust. The helicopter crew emptied a bottle of mineral water and dried it. With a cap on it, they threw it down to me. I tried to get as much as possible of the dust into the bottle. Then I hid it under my diving suit before the Norwegian fleet arrived. I took the bottle home with me and fell into oblivion."

"I understand," said Erik Fenton.

It was the remains of Erik, the Viking. The Nameless one prevented his dust from being blown away. That's why the Viking couldn't come to Walhall. He has yet to fulfill his service to him.

"Where is the dust now?" Erik Fenton asked the general.

"I must have moved it somewhere. Perhaps the bottle is in my garage, where everything is mixed up."

"General," Erik was angry. "Look for this bottle and bring it to me. I don't care how you'd do it. I need the dust. The future of the earth is at stake."

The general held his cell phone in his hand and set a number. The contact came about, "Mr. Dumbler" were his words.

Then he gave the order to look for the bottle and bring it to him. He also asked other questions. Then he hung up. Erik walked back and forth in the apartment and went into the bathroom. It was upstairs next to the bedroom. He stood in front of the mirror, took off his shirt and got cut from accidentally touching the edge of the sink. It hurt a little. The blood stopped and he disinfected the wounds. He washed his hands in the sink and let the water glide over his hands. It felt cold. He also moistened his face and looked in the mirror above the sink. The water dripped down. It seemed as if he looked through his eyes. Even though he felt uncomfortable, he was aware of what he had to do.

Then he put on another shirt, which he took out of his closet. He also put on other trousers. He put the short cotton trousers and the dirty and blood-soaked shirt in the laundry basket. Then he walked down the stairs. As he walked down the stairs leading into the living room, he felt lonely. He missed his family. But for this mission, he had to go alone. He saw the general standing in the living room.

"How is my family?" he asked.

"I asked when I had Mr. Dumbler on the phone. They're fine. They've arrived in a safe place. Should there be a war here, they will be kept up to date. Every surveillance team is out there and the transmissions are disseminated from us."

"There will be war. Do what I have to say immediately."

The General swallowed. Would the aliens attack, even if the black arrow was only a warning?

"Just say the word," he asked.

"All fighter planes available worldwide should be in the air before sunrise. I will try to stop the invaders to some extent until then all should be prepared."

"You? Stop them? How's that supposed to happen?"

"I will be active shortly. I have the power of the Nameless within me. Not all power, but enough to be a help in this battle. Stay in the house. I will go into the garden and prepare myself."

Erik Fenton walked to the glass door and opened it. With a few steps, he was at the pool and walked on. He glided gently over the freshly cut lawn. He stopped in the middle and looked into the dark sky. Would he be able to stop the invaders? He was convinced of it. Meanwhile, General Rock phoned and carried out Erik Fenton's instructions.

Chapter 53

Ministry of Defense headquarters. Gibbs agitatedly walked into the middle of the room.

"General Rock has just sent us a message," Ted Gibbs said to the others in the room. He was standing at the top of the stairs looking at the employees. There was silence. Everyone wanted to hear this man speak. "There will be war. This information is not a hoax. This war causes every fighter pilot to be in the air before sunrise and to be implemented worldwide effective immediately."

Then, he turned around and disappeared into the conference hall. He grabbed the handset and dialed a number. Government official James Bloom was briefed and he passed the information onto the President.

Chapter 54

The earth turned slowly and the morning came. The darkness gave way and the first sunbeam arose. That was the sign the beings had been waiting for. Everyone knew what to do. They activated their devastating deadly projectiles and were ready to destroy the earth. In the strange spaceship, a jerk went through the figure.

"I feel Him. I feel the presence of my cursed brother in this low-life planet. He's up to something. But what? I will find out, brother."

Chapter 55

Near the Canadian border. Mr. Dumbler drove the car through a forest and let the car roll out in front of a lattice bridle. There was also the lattice gate. 'NO PASSAGE. MILITARY AREA' was written on a red sign, which was attached to the gate. He honked his horn briefly and two armed, uniformed soldiers came out of the thicket.

"This is where my companionship ends. One of these men will accompany you safely through the area. Please get out now."

The family did as they were told. With their luggages in hand, they stood in front of the gate and waited. Mr. Dumbler drove the car back and disappeared from their sight. The family was accompanied through the thicket and stopped at a bunker entrance. It was still dark and the soldier pointed his flashlight at the entrance. A small box was inside the wall. To enter, one must input a numerical code, as with an ATM. The soldier's fingers were nimble and the entrance opened. The door opened quietly and the family entered. It was an elevator that carried people into the depths. The soldier stayed outside and disappeared. The elevator went down and the Fenton family was not comfortable at all. The ride ended and the doors of the elevator opened. Another soldier greeted the family.

"Would you please follow me?" a remark that was a statement

rather than a request. And so, they followed him quietly.

The uniformed man led them through a labyrinth of concrete passages. Some men, also in uniform, passed by and greeted him. These people disappeared into other branches. The family went further and got into a surprisingly comfortable yet cozy room. This room was equipped with bunk beds. There was a bathroom to the left of the entrance and a small living room to the right. They placed their hand luggages next to the beds and immediately stepped into the living room. The family sat down on the sofa. They sat together and stared at a wall. Mikael walked nervously back and forth.

His mother said, "Sit down, Michael."

"I can't, Mom. I am nervous. What are we supposed to do here? Uncertainty gnaws at me. I don't know what is going on out there. I don't know what's going to happen to Dad."

"We don't know either," Helen Fenton said. "even I don't know how your father is doing."

"Yes... Dad," Irina murmured. "I am afraid for him. Is he still trapped in the bright light?"

"The light. Is it really from an alien?" Andy asked.

"The Nameless One is a powerful being. It will help your father. I am very sure of that."

Mikael walked to a piece of furniture. This was in the corner. He reached into the upper drawer, which was half open. He pulled out a remote control.

"Here," he said and showed it to the family.

Without asking, he pressed a button. The wall opened in the middle and a widescreen TV came out automatically. Mikael pressed a button again and the TV turned on. Each TV station showed something. The usual television programs. Few channels were only available from the military. Through the satellites, they could see everything worldwide. Everything was still quiet. But after half an hour, they knew more. With frightened expressions, they saw what was going on.

"That is your father who ignited this. I'm sure of it. May the Nameless One protect him," Helen said to himself.

Chapter 56

More than half an hour passed when General Rock stepped up to the glass door and opened it. "Mr. Fenton," he said. "I gave the order. All available fighters are in the air. It was confirmed to me. What happens now?"

Erik Fenton stood on the lawn and looked at the man. "In a few minutes, I will be ready. Go inside and close your eyes."

The general did as he was called to do. Since he was still holding the mobile phone in his hand, he wanted to capture the scene with it. He lifted it up and let the recording run. But this was of no use. He wouldn't see anything on it later. But he didn't know that yet. Erik Fenton just stood there. First, a light illuminated on his legs, then it flooded his whole body. Erik shone in a bright light, like it could blind someone by one look. It reached so far. What came now changed the world for a short time.

Chapter 57

Space. The being in the other room spoke to the leader. It said, "I have an even bigger source of energy here than I did before. There is something wrong, captain."

"I feel it," he said. "Quick! Send a message to everyone else. They should make a move. None of the spaceships may stand still. No!"

But this order came too late for some of their forces.

Chapter 58

Erik Fenton sucked in the air. General Rock slowly backed away from the glass door and watched the scene unfold. He was still holding his phone in his hand and is running the recording. At the same time, with the snow-covered mountains, in the spaceship, the Nameless had confided something to Fenton. Now the time had come to reveal it. It was the name of the Nameless One. Erik blew out the air and shouted it against the sky. A tremendous energy of light came out of his mouth and raced towards the sky. It was like a sword blow, cutting the darkness. The ray shot into the earth's atmosphere and lay like a protective cloak around the round sphere. The sky, the blue sky that was seen every day, disappeared. The ray continued to shoot and captured several spaceships in orbit. They exploded and fell as glowing objects down to Earth. The beam continued its way and disappeared into the dark universe.

Exhausted by this cry, Erik Fenton tilted forward and kneeled on the ground. He leaned on his arms to support himself. The lawn was soft under his fingers. He breathed deeply. This cry had demanded a lot of his strength. The light around him became weaker, but it did not disappear. He looked to the left towards the glass door. The general came out slowly behind it. The color had disappeared from his face. He had taken his phone down before. Erik Fenton nodded to him before whispering something.

"It is done. I was able to stop it a little. Now it's your turn."

The general nodded and looked up at the sky. It slowly became bright and the sun brought the first rays. He saw the first fighter planes fly by and something else. It flashed and thundered. Fire rained from the sky. The war had begun.

Chapter 59

In the Ministry of Defense. "Sir," someone called from the hall. The "Sir," was heard and Ted Gibbs looked at the monitors. The main screen was the most important. What he and everyone in the room saw was incredible. The Earth's atmosphere changed and was enveloped in a blinding right light.

"What's going on?" he thought in a low voice.

"Sir!" shouted again the man from the middle, "I have located the source of the energy. It comes from the place where General Rock is."

"Is this energy source dangerous to us?"

"As I see it, Sir, it's not. It surrounds the whole planet and I don't know how, but it seems to protect us."

Ted Gibbs thought briefly.

"Are the surveillance satellites still online?"

"Yes, Sir."

"Show me a recording from above, please. I want to know what's going on out there."

The recording was rewound and everyone could see what a devastating effect the energy source had. A bright beam ate through space and captured some spaceships. These were completely shredded and the ray disappeared into the black air void mass.

"Wow! That's really something," muttered someone from the hall.

"Exactly," said Ted Gibbs. "The energy beam has shot some off. We have a reinforcement. Now it's up to us to act quickly. The weapon systems on the communication satellites are switched on. Let's wait for a sign. Then we'll press the buttons. Prepare everything."

It was even more hectic than before.

Chapter 60

In a space in the universe. "That damned one!" shouted the creature in the spaceship. "He almost caught me. Come on, give the order to shoot. Destroy them all! How dare he!"

The other being in the room pressed a button and the signal was transmitted. All spaceships shot at the earth. But the impacts were missing. All projectiles bounced off the earth's atmosphere. It was the energy of the Nameless that stopped it. An absolute shield.

"We cannot get through with the projectiles. This energy protects the atmosphere. What should we do?"

"Give the signal to attack. Aar Kar should be the first to fly through the atmosphere. Elo-Ko and his troops should go to the earth's surface as ordered."

"Aar Kar goes first? He is the strongest of all." The hated one hissed.

The being in the other room understood and gave the signal. Aar Kar set his huge spaceship on course to Earth. Dull, soaked in cotton wool, his voice sounded. His face was full of pustules and thick warts. A horrible spongy creature.

"Destroy. Everything."

It spoke to itself. It sounded like it, but it was an order to its kind. The spaceship approached the Earth's atmosphere and penetrated through it. Aar Kar felt safe to destroy these earth dwellers. But the shield of the Nameless one put a line through his bill. The entire protective device, the protective shield, failed. His energy absorbed everything and strengthened the earth's atmosphere. Aar Kar was vulnerable. He condemned this shield and said: "Spread out. Destroy everything,". Now he had fully come through and activated his spaceship. This huge spaceship consisted of thousands of small particles. Aar Kar pressed the last button and the spaceship burst apart. All the particles became small space fliers. Each was fully active with the same body as Aar Kar.

The space pilots spread out in the sky and opened fire to the earth. Nobody had counted on resistance. Like falcons, which spotted the prey, the jet pilots and fighter bombers of the Airforce collapsed over the intruders. The sky filled with explosions.

Chapter 61

The phone rang. General Rock called. "Yes, Mr. Dumbler?"

"Sir. I'm at your house. Your wife had me rummage through the garage. I found the bottle. But what worries me is that I can't leave. The airspace is closed. How do I proceed, Sir?"

"I'll get back to you. Stay there."

General Rock cut the connection. He looked at the kneeling man. "Mr. Fenton? Are you all right?"

"A little weak. I just got a little old for these things."

"What was that?" asked the general. "What did you do?"

"A rampart around the earth. The Nameless one will protect us for some time."

Erik Fenton rose slowly. As soon as he stood on his feet again, he approached the general.

"Do you have what I need?"

"Mr. Dumbler found the bottle. But he has a problem. He can't come here. The airspace is closed."

"It is enough for me if you tell me exactly where he is. I will go there. But I still need a moment." Erik went into the house and came out with a sword in his hand. "For safety," he said.

The general gave him all the information. The glow around Erik's body have not yet ceased. It intensified again and Erik Fenton disappeared before the eyes of the general. He stopped and looked at the empty lawn. After a few minutes, he informed Mr. Dumbler.

"Mr. Fenton may show up at your place."

"He already did. He glowed, took the bottle and disappeared before my eyes."

"Good. Stay with my wife until I call again."

Then General Rock interrupted the connection.

"Who knows where he is right now."

Chapter 62

Universe. The message from Aar Kar had arrived. He had spread out and attacked the earth, but he needed help. The creature in the spaceship gave the others the order to attack before he spoke to the other allies.

"Support Aar Kar. Turn off the shields. These would cost us too much energy and strengthen my brother nemesis." Everyone did this and set themselves in motion. They immediately felt that this was a mistake to deactivate the shields.

Chapter 63

Ministry of Defense. "Sir." The person addressed was Ted Gibbs.

"What is it?"

"I have something here. It looks like all the unidentified objects have deactivated their shields. The readings indicate it. There's no energy available."

"They're attacking Earth. This is our opportunity to stop some."

"Everything's ready, Sir."

Ted Gibbs took a deep breath. If he gave the order now, there was no going back.

"God help us."

He took a little break and said, "press the damn button."

The man at work was sweating. He didn't feel well. But he had to carry out the command. Between the countless small lamps and buttons, he lifted a plastic disc. Below it was a red button. He pressed it with the palm of his hand and the alarm went off. Everyone present could see through the outside cameras what was going on in space. The weapon systems of the communication satellites received the signals. These were distributed around the globe. The silent clicking could not be heard in space and the projectiles detached themselves from the communication satellites. The nuclear missiles had some targets.

Chapter 64

Somewhere in the Universe, a creature hissed in the other room.

"What is it?" asked the leader.

"These things in orbit got a signal from the planet. It looks as if something has been activated."

"What has been activated?" hissed the leader.

"It's... ." The answer didn't get any further.

The being in the other room started the spaceship and flew a loop, only inches away from what came to them. The nuclear missiles found their target on some spaceships. There were some silent explosions. Huge fire broke out and spread in the bright atmosphere of the earth. Then the fires broke off abruptly as they were not fed oxygen. Metal shreds and larger chunks of the spaceships shot through the endless vastness of space.

Elo-Ko landed on the Earth's surface with countless spaceships. Landing all over the United States and other nearby countries, not only in New York. He distributed his ground troops all over the world. Terrible creatures, armed with destructive weapons, were attacking the soldiers. After a few minutes, many earth soldiers had fallen in battle. These alien beings were invincible. What they did not know was that they had enemies who taught them fear.

Chapter 65

Walhall. Odin sat on his throne. Suddenly, he flinched. He stood up silently and grabbed his sword, which stood leaning against his throne. No words were uttered. His men knew that it's time to go to the entrance gate. One by one, they walked through the great hall and reached the gate. Two men pushed the door apart so that everyone could walk through. Odin was the last to step through the wooden door. His gaze wandered from left to right. What he saw pleased him. Previously, the square in front of Walhall's gates had been empty. Now some figures stood in front of it.

With a powerful voice, he spoke to them, "Warrior! Faithful Viking warriors. The moment has come. We will use our weapons for the last time and destroy the enemy in all countries where they are. The Nameless One will protect us. Bring death to the enemies." He cried out the last sentence.

As he raised his sword high above him, his last words were outbid by wild shouting. Before Odin stood hundreds of thousands of Viking warriors killed in war. They all raised their weapons and shouted out their battle cry. Then they turned around, walked to the stone bridge and crossed it. Soon, the divine fog had swallowed all the warriors.

Chapter 66

Back in the Ministry of Defense headquarters. A soldier asked his commander, "Sir?"

"Yes?" Ted Gibbs said.

"It has been reported that many of our soldiers were killed and other nation's soldiers were also killed worldwide. These alien troops have devastating weapons. We are becoming fewer and fewer. I'm afraid we're outnumbered, Sir. If not, a miracle happens, then...," he did not speak further.

Everybody in the room was thinking. *'What can I do?'* Ted Gibbs thought. He had no solution. Suddenly, there was a bang and it sounded doubled. The chair was tilted backwards and hit the ground. That was because the man on the monitor jumped open like a snake.

"What is it?"

"The systems are going crazy. Just like last time. It's showing me an energy that I have already experienced."

In front of the eyes of those present, a fog formed which should not be there at all.

"The outside cameras are on. Let's have a look," said Gibbs.

The man at the monitor was sitting on his chair again and pressed the buttons. Everyone could see the incomprehensible.

"This is the miracle we have been waiting for! Let everyone know. We have reinforcements!"

Chapter 67

Elo-Kos's ground troops were surprised by the fog. They couldn't do anything but be surrounded by it. They became witnesses when the ground trembled, and opened with a *Bang!* An enormous hole and furrows were made. They didn't know what caused this earthquake. Only when the fog cleared did they see what it was about. A strange being came out. It looked like a human, but this one had strange clothes on and a giant unlike the other soldiers. In his hand, he held a huge hammer. It was Thor who had his hammer hit the ground. This little trick of his gained the attention of the enemies. Behind him, other armed figures slowly appeared. Upon the new warriors' arrival, there was one thing on their minds: It was time to bring death to these strangers.

The Horde shouted "Odin," and "Thor," and threw themselves death-defyingly against the Ungudds. Thor and Odin were the first to attack. Odin swung a sword over his head and pushed it down. The alien had no way to avoid it. The stroke divided it into two halves. Thor swung his hammer and hit the enemies. Due to the impact, the alien flew away in a high arc. Only now did the Ungudds shot at the Vikings, but to no avail. The fired charges bounced off their bodies. The Nameless one protected the Vikings with his light. Thus, the aliens, without using their weapons, had to attack them head-on. But with what? They only have these firearms. No swords, knives or axes. Therefore, in a desperate attempt, they carelessly fired the useless weapons. The Vikings left nothing burning. Like a plague of locusts, they've overrun the field. None of the Ungudds stopped.

"Let us help the others in the field," Odin shouted and all disappeared in the light and fog.

The faces of the soldiers remained bewildered. No one could explain what had just happened here. But it was not important as they had won this fight and shouted their victory out loud. The time came when a high-ranking officer gave the order.

"Clear these scums away. Burn everything. Collect the weapons and go to the others. Help where you can. Come on, let's go. Move!"

Chapter 68

Aar Kar lost many flying machines. Without the vast aircrafts he boasted about, he became weaker. The fighter planes helplessly defended their airspace. They fired everything they had at their disposal. New York had become a battlefield. Be it in the air or on the ground. Even so, it was more dangerous on the ground. Countless machines caught on fire and turned the streets into hell. Explosions, cries of the civilian population and the soldiers were the result. One house after the other ceased to exist. The soldiers tried to defeat Elo-Kos's ground troops, without success. But this battle was not for them.

A fog formed and a man came out with an ordinary-looking bottle. Everyone looked at him in amazement. He stopped his steps, opened the lid and tilted the contents to the ground. It was the ashes of Erik, the Viking. The ashes began to glow and formed into the complete body of a giant.

What they did not know was that the face of the Viking manifested itself again on the dragon boat. This was due to the fact that Erik, the Viking, has not step foot in Walhall yet. He was floating for a long time, as a spirit, in the intermediate world. If he had been in Walhall, then all the Vikings would have proceeded in the afterlife and nobody would be there to kill these aliens. The two looked at each other.

"Are you ready?" asked Erik Fenton.

"For over 25 years," said his ancestor, bouncing his axe.

A heavy voice sounded behind them, "We will be at your side."

From the fog, Odin, Thor and many other Viking warriors appeared. Erik, the Viking, fell reverently on his knees.

"Rise, Erik. Through your deeds and bravery, you deserve our honor. We will fight beside you. Let us begin."

"Attack!" screamed the Viking and ran for the enemy troops.

Erik Fenton couldn't stand it either and ran with the deities on the Ungudds. He shouted out the names "Odin," and "Thor," and swung his sword.

Chapter 69

The TV in the bunker's been on for hours. All cameras were on and everyone in the Fenton family could follow in the action.

"I can't watch it anymore," Irina said. "These aliens kill our species one by one. Our soldiers have no chance. Turn it off." Helen Fenton screamed and pressed her hand in front of her mouth when Andy held the remote control of her hand and wanted to switch it off.

"Don't," she said. "Look."

Everyone looked at the running pictures. Fog had appeared on the battlefield out of nowhere. A man stepped out of it. He held a bottle in his hand and emptied the contents onto the ground.

"That's Dad," said Irina. "What is he doing?"

"He dumped some sand or ashes on the floor and even carries a sword with him," said Mikael.

The three understood nothing more.

"What is that," whispered Andy.

The sand formed a giant creature they didn't know.

Only Helen explained, "It is Erik, the Viking. He saved my life back then. He is your father's ancestor."

In their faces, the unbelievable and incomprehensible was written. They looked on the television with excitement.

"Dad stands with his ancestor before this pack of aliens. Does he really think he can stop them?" said Mikael.

Helen said "Look at the fog. The two are not alone."

Out of the fog, countless Viking warriors emerged, who soon ran away towards their enemies.

"Our dad is a warrior and a hero at the same time," Irina screamed and had tears in her eyes.

Like everyone else in the room, she was afraid of losing him.

Chapter 70

General Rock was taken by a military jeep to a mobile station and could follow everything that was happening through the monitor. The monitor was connected to the central station.

"Unbelievable," he said. "This is Fenton. What is he doing? Where did he get these many strong fighters from? Quick, get me a helicopter ready. I want to be there."

Before he was ready, he watched everything closely and witnessed this attack.

Chapter 71

Back in the Ministry of Defense headquarters. "This is impossible," said the man at the desk. He stared at the monitor and pressed some buttons. He turned around.

He shouted, "Sir," and silence befell the room.

Everyone looked at the main screen and watched what happened.

"What is this," Ted Gibbs asked.

"I don't know. It looks like the black matter is condensing into space."

Everybody kept looking eagerly. Where the shining stars were, there was nothing more to be seen. It looked like a black hole. The black hole began to glow at the edges. It became brighter and brighter until the black hole no longer existed. It shone brightly and something appeared out of it. It was a huge bright spaceship and it wasn't alone. Behind it, thousands of small flying objects peeled out. As soon as they were seen, they flew in all directions — distributed around the whole planet and behind the enemy spaceships, which wanted to penetrate into the earth's atmosphere.

These spacecrafts fired on the enemies. Thousands and thousands of flying machines clashed against each other. This space fight was hell. The first bright spaceship was not the only one. Soon more than eight hundred big and small crafts came behind it from the black hole. However, they stayed motionless in space and did not attack. What this meant, they did not know.

"I do not understand. What is going on here? What kind of mighty spaceships are they, standing in space?"

None of those present could do anything. None of them knew anything.

"I suspect that the first bright spaceship is the lead. Let's see what it does next," said Ted Gibbs.

Chapter 72

Inside the command center of the malicious spaceship, the aliens are discussing their reports on the situation.

"My sensors indicate an energy source. It comes from sector B2X. It indicates to me that the earth shield is slowly weakening. It's as if the energy surrounding the planet is flowing into sector B2X. This is our chance to fire everything at the planet," said an Ungudd.

"A black hole is opening up."

A bright spaceship appeared, and the alien hissed hatefully into the room. "My brother deceived me. He was not on earth. He appeared behind us and wants his power back. Let's send him a greeting. Fire on his spaceship and the fire the rest on Earth. Let them all suffer."

Unfortunately, the fired projectiles did mostly no harm. They just bounced off. But some hit the earth's surface. The detonations were to be seen everywhere. They looked like little mushrooms sprouting.

The ground beneath the feet of the warriors trembled. Something had happened. They looked up at the sky and saw a bright light heading towards the earth. The enemy spaceship fired its deadly cargo. Houses exploded; whole blocks of flats simply no longer existed. The end seemed near when it suddenly stopped. No one knew why.

Chapter 73

During the flight, General Rock looked at everything on a monitor. They flew, for safety, at ground level, not to be hit. Nothing escaped him. More and more Viking warriors appeared and plunged into battle. In many countries, these warriors have been victorious and therefore no longer needed. They disappeared into the light and reappeared here in New York. The hundreds of thousands of warriors were united and fought a fierce battle with Elo-Kos's ground troops. The jets flew around and continued to fire their charges. The entire airspace was filled with explosions. Aar Kar's hostile spaceships soon ceased to exist. Only a few were still buzzing around. The being was weakened and was vulnerable. The last space plane was shot down. He was now alone and couldn't escape anymore. The jet pilots flew to him.

"We Earthlings salute you," one of them said the words, and everyone fired on Aar Kar's spaceship.

The huge explosion could not be overlooked. His shredded spaceship crashed on New York and buried hundreds of houses. A sea of flames spread. Everyone nearby burned in an instant. It was hell on earth.

Chapter 74

Aar Kar has been defeated. It no longer exists," said the being. "Our allies have been decimated. We cannot escape. Even Elo-Kos's ground troops are becoming fewer. We still need our energy. Shall we stop attacking Earth?"

The leader raged and nodded. "This is all my brother's fault. If there is no way out, we will fly to him and steer my spaceship into his. Let's see how he will react," it said hatefully.

'That won't be necessary, brother' it heard a voice.

It was the Nameless man who spoke to him intellectually.

'Let's meet on earth. Just the two of us.'

"I will come and kill you, brother," the being played out the words and went to a space glider. It made its way to earth immediately.

A glider also detached itself from the bright spaceship and followed it. As soon as they were through the earth's shield, the enemy spaceship detonated. The Nameless had previously given the order to shoot it down, as the shields no longer held. There was nothing more hostile in the room. Everything had been destroyed. Only the hated brother remained standing and he cried out. Now he had no chance to get away. He armed himself with everything at his disposal. A duel was imminent, and his brother was to die today.

Chapter 75

Death to the Unguuds," Odin shouted and swung his sword. The ground battle went on for a few moments and then it was over. There were no more Elo-Kos's ground troops. Elo-Ko's spaceship was also put to an end.

"Victory is ours," Odin shouted at the warriors.

"Thor," and "Odin," were the response of the warriors.

All swung their weapons above their height. The victory was theirs. Everyone would remember this honorable last fight. Erik Fenton stood in the midst of the warriors. His ancestor was right next to him. His gaze was directed upwards. He saw everyone else approaching them, including two alien space gliders.

"Move aside. Make way," said Fenton. "Something is coming towards us. Don't attack and keep calm."

The space gliders were silent as they approached the group. The only noise was a helicopter approaching and landing not far from them.

Chapter 76

General Rock took a worried look at the city of New York. This city was almost non-existent, like a ghost town. Something was burning everywhere and many houses, even skyscrapers were no longer standing. Dirt and dust, blood and tears were the only things that can be found. It hurt every person who had lost everything here. The helicopter landed and the rotors whirled everything up. As soon as it stood on the ground, the doors opened and General Rock got out. He slowly stepped towards the group of warriors. Some soldiers were also there. His target was Erik Fenton.

The doors of the space gliders opened and the enemy skinned mutt came out of one of them. "I can't believe it," said Erik Fenton in surprise.

"That is not possible. It's still alive," his ancestor made the comment.

The giant growled and wanted to jump on the alien.

Erik Fenton held him back. "Wait."

The Nameless man appeared from the other door. He approached his brother, brightly shining.

"Let's put an end to this once and for all," he said.

"Yes. You will meet your end today," hissed the evil being.

"Let us begin."

The two brothers approached. Both had drawn their weapons and were already about to attack each other when a voice interrupted them.

"Stop," Erik Fenton had spoken. The two stopped. "What do this man want from you? It's my fault that it all happened here. I have awakened you. The warriors and your brother," he said to the Nameless.

"What does this wretch want," hissed the horrible being.

The Nameless one spoke nothing, only looked at Erik Fenton and nodded.

"This is now my fight. Put down the box around your stomach, deactivate all energy and face me. I won't accept any assistance from your brother either. I am free of everything. Are you confident or are you just a coward?" Erik said, swinging his sword in his right hand. In his left hand, he held a knife. His ancestor had pressed it into his hand. The Nameless man stepped aside and gave up his place.

"When I'm done with this wretch, it's your turn, brother."

Chapter 77

Countless military helicopters hover over the whole city. Everything was carefully controlled. The chances that there are more aliens hiding was feasible. In between, some helicopters from the TV and radio stations floated around and captured the scenes live. One of these TV stations was near the scene. The Fenton family sat spellbound in front of the TV and watched what happened.

"I can't believe it. There's Dad and his ancestor," said Mikael.

"What is he up to?" asked Irina.

"I don't know," the mother said. "I only hope that he knows what he is doing."

She screamed when she saw what was happening. Everyone was queasy in their stomach area. Something happened that they never dreamed of.

Chapter 78

The enemy thought he was safe. He could kill this man in a matter of seconds. As soon as he had the box around his belly, he took his weapons in his hand. He felt so confident that he had not expected the actions of Erik Fenton. The being was unprotected and Erik took advantage of it. With full force, he hurled the sword towards the alien and hit his chest. It penetrated and came out at the back. Then, Erik ran off and jumped on the being. It tilted with its back on the ground. Erik pressed his foot on its chest and cut its throat with the knife. Black blood splashed up like a fountain and wetted Erik's body. At that moment, everything else didn't matter. Fenton wanted to kill this being. It couldn't even defend itself and died. Its head lay to the side and the tongue hung out. The last of its race, except the Nameless one, didn't exist anymore. Erik pulled his sword out of its body and struck one last time. He separated the head from its body.

"We are now safe from their grasp," he said, turning to the Horde and walking towards them. A thousand victorious screams were the result. The Viking warriors praised Erik Fenton. They showed their respect and raised their weapons.

"Here, you'll need it," spoke to his ancestor and handed him the knife. He accepted it gratefully.

"That was wise of you to act so fast," said the giant and put it into his trouser belt. Their voices sank when they saw that the Nameless man was walking towards them.

"You fought well, Erik Fenton. Even without my aid, you managed to kill my brother. I am now the last one of my race. The power from my brother has come to me and thus made me more powerful than before. Does it bother you?"

"No. I have always had faith in you. All these warriors as well. Why else would we follow else would we follow you? You have helped us and we thank you for it."

"You have answered wisely, but you do not know me completely. What I have to say will frighten you to death. Are you ready for it? Are you ready to experience the truth in three days?"

Erik Fenton swallowed hard. He didn't know what the Nameless one was up to. "Whatever may come. I will stand by you," he said. "But first, I would like to clarify something."

"Speak," the Nameless one agreed.

"At that time, the spaceship flew with your brother into the vastness of space and with him many injured Viking warriors. It was said that the spaceship would explode. So, your brother would've already be dead and we could have saved ourselves. The whole country is a debris field. What has happened? How did your brother come back?"

Before the Nameless man had the chance to answer back, General Rock came closer and joined behind Fenton. The Viking horde listened intently to the Nameless man's voice as they wanted to know.

"I saw it coming," began the Nameless One. "I had seen the future and had to act. I let you believe that it was all over. My brother was in the spaceship with the warriors. The Vikings locked him up in a room where he couldn't escape. Everyone said that the spaceship would explode someday. It was a miscalculation. I didn't let it happen and freed my brother. With my thoughts, I opened the door lock and let him go. The injured Vikings who could hardly stand were killed by him with honor. After that, he flew on and disappeared into nowhere for a long time."

"You did what?" screamed Erik, the Viking, and swung his axe. "You had my men killed without a fight?"

"They were already dead even before they went on the spaceship," he said. "You knew that."

"Calm down," said Erik Fenton. "He had his reasons," and stood in the way of his ancestor.

"That's the way it is," the Nameless man continued. "As I said, I had taken a look into the future and it looked gloomy in the worst way possible. I don't want to say any further. In three days, I will explain to you all, to all mankind the truth why all of this happened here. Bring all the statesmen and women together. Tell me where it is best for you, I will go there. Until then," he took a breather. "Keep calm. The man behind you," he said to General Rock, "will take care of everything. Rock, Pull out all your soldiers and fighter planes. It's over. There are thousands of fighters in orbit who are there for your safety and over eight hundred other spaceships. They serve a purpose that I will soon bring to your knowledge. Do not be afraid. Pass on my message. Erik Fenton will contact me where the meeting point will be."

The Nameless man turned around, stepped to his glider and flew back to his bright spaceship. Through the thoughts of the being, the other glider flew after him. Until now, the Viking's God had not made himself felt. But now he stepped up to Erik Fenton.

Odin spoke to him in a heavy voice. "We have come together through the power of the Nameless. It was an honor for me to speak with you and fight together. We will talk about you for ages to come. You are always welcome to us, even in the distant future with your future lives."

"Odin, I thank you and your brave warriors. I will also tell my people about you. You will never be forgotten. My children and their children will pass this on. It is a promise."

"Farewell, Erik Fenton."

"Farewell, you gods and warriors from Walhall."

Erik raised his arm for the last greeting. Then the spirits disappeared never to be seen again in the fog that had formed shortly before. He lowered his arm again, turned around and looked into the long faces of the men.

"What was that?" whispered General Rock.

"Well, they were my allies. They were the gods from Walhall. Odin, Thor and all the other brave Viking warriors."

"Odin and Thor?! I can't believe it."

Fenton responded nothing and turned to his ancestor. Erik, the Viking, stood beside him. "Your work is finished. It's time for you to follow your God. He will honor you like everyone else before you."

The giant looked down on Erik Fenton. "I thank you. It is the second time that we say goodbye. This time for good."

They hugged each other. The giant then stepped towards the fog and disappeared into it. Erik turned to the general.

"Can I get a free flight home?" he asked.

"The army doesn't carry civilians, but of course I'll make an exception with you," he said.

"Thank you."

"You're welcome. Without you, Mr. Fenton, who knows what would have happened? The world is in your debt."

"Hmm.... maybe. But I don't trust that we have claimed peace yet. Let's see what the Nameless one has in mind."

"Yes. For now, let us fly you all home. I will take care of your family personally. We'll see you soon," and greeted you militarily.

Erik Fenton went to the military helicopter and soon he left the village. General Rock ordered the soldiers to secure everything. Also, to clean up the remnants of chaos. The stinking body of the aliens lay unchanged on the ground and slowly dissolved into a black pool. He phoned Ted Gibbs.

"All clear. Everything is under control and we have triumphed. Withdraw all fighter jets back to base. The ground troops should control the roads and other areas. As for space, the spaceships in orbit are not hostile to us. But keep your eyes open."

He cut the wire and set off. A small military helicopter stood further ahead. This brought him home.

Chapter 79

Back in the Ministry of Defense headquarters, Ted Gibbs had just received General Rock's orders and hung up.

"It's finally over," Ted Gibbs declared and the hall turned into a party. Everyone cheered and threw themselves into each other's arms. They all shook their hands and patted each other on their shoulders.

"General Rock has worked a miracle. That was a tactical risk, but also an absolutely wise decision to call in the civilian. My respect for this general has increased tenfold."

Many in the hall were able to hear and confirm that. Ted called the President of the United States of America and told him everything. As soon as he had hung up, a member of the staff called through the monitor.

"Sir."

"What's up?"

"Our fighter jets have passed from heaven. Everything is quiet. I mean too calm," and pointed to the monitor.

"What is that," said Ted Gibbs.

"The smaller spaceships that helped us on outer space seems to be assembling. Something is going on. They hover over us as if they are watching us. First one sector, then they move to another."

"Strange," said Ted Gibbs. "Keep your eyes open."

"What is that," exclaimed another employee in the corner loudly. "Sir, come quickly."

Gibbs hurried to this employee. "What's the matter?" he asked.

"I programmed this on my own. Apparently, someone is hacking into our system. It retrieves data from all weapon systems and locations. Also, from the prisons of the country, bank accounts and the population. Everything in the computer. If it doesn't deceive me, it's not just us. I believe worldwide."

"Cut that. Quickly."

"I've already tried it. It doesn't work. Even if I pulled the plug, it doesn't stop."

"Damn," called Ted Gibbs. "What is going on here."

He called the President immediately and gave his report. *"Don't do anything yet. Leave it as it is. I believe we will soon have an explanation. But continue to secure what you can."*

"Yes, Sir," and the call was hung up.

'What is coming towards us?' he asked himself.

Chapter 80

The day after. The Fenton family was accompanied from the safe bunker. After a few hours of flying, they reached their home in the late afternoon. Erik Fenton was waiting for them. As soon as they got out of the helicopter, they ran towards the house. The kids ahead hugged their father. Helen came right after them, hugged her husband and kissed him. "I was so afraid for you," she whispered with tears in her eyes.

"Everything is good," said Erik. "We should just look forward from now on. Come on, let's go into the house. We can talk better there."

They entered the house and closed the door. The noise of the helicopter can still be heard, but soon no more. They disappeared into the clouds and a satisfied grin lay on General Rock's face. He had brought the family home safely. His next destination was the White House.

"Dad," cried Irina and hugged her father. Her tears ran down his cheeks and moistened his dirty shirt.

The two sons joined him. "I was so afraid for you, dad, and so were mom and my siblings. But now we have you back safe and sound. Thank God."

"Where did you learn to fight like that? Who was your trainer? How did you know the Vikings?"

"Well...I trained daily with the sword in secret. I had the feeling that nothing was over since last time. I learned the tactics in an intermediate dimension from my ancestor Erik, the Viking. His horde stood aside when the invaders landed on earth for the first time. I could handle the other weapons before. Years ago, I was a policeman in New York and cleaned up the streets from criminal. But now enough with the stories. Let's go to sleep. I am tired from the fights. You understand?"

Helen stepped up to her husband and looked him in the eye. She knew him too well. "There is still something there. Something that occupies you. Isn't there?"

"How could I deceive you, wife. How often you are right. Yes, something is still there. In two days, a meeting will take place. The Nameless one will speak to the politicians and the rest of the world. What it is, I don't know yet."

"It can wait. Come now and let's go to sleep," she said and went into the bedroom.

As soon as Erik lay in bed, he fell into a deep sleep. He didn't notice Helen undressing him and putting the blanket over his body. She whimpered secretly. Not only did she have her beloved husband back, but she also saw the wounds the guard had inflicted on his body after Walhall. She soon joined him and fell asleep. The kids were still very excited and stayed in the living room. Irina was drinking a fruit juice and a beer for the young men. They deserved it. Such excitement was rare.

"This is a fact," Andy said. "Our father is a hero."

"Yes, and a good killer at that," said Mikael. "Did you see him swing his sword and kill one alien after another? Even the aliens found a quick death." His gaze wandered to the sword which lay on the ground. "Should I?" he whispered.

"Let it be. It is his sword. Only he may touch it, ok," Irina spoke.

"Yes, I agree," said Mikael.

They spoke a little bit and a little later, they also seized into exhaustion. Soon, there was peace and quiet in the house.

Chapter 81

The General's helicopter landed at a later hour on the sacred lawn in front of the White House. He got out and walked inside. He was accompanied into the oval room and the President appeared immediately. He was joined by Ted Gibbs.

He began to speak, "General Rock. You have given our nation and the world an invaluable victory. We, the people and I, would like to thank you for your service."

"It was wise to call in a civilian. This Erik Fenton was the greatest help we could ever have. If it hadn't been for him and those strange warriors, who knows what could have happened to us," said Ted Gibbs.

"Indeed," the President murmured. "But we still have a problem to solve. These hackers are attacking our national system. Who is responsible for this?"

"We don't know yet. Let's wait and see what happens in two days," said Ted Gibbs.

"I agree with you. The Nameless one will speak to us. Do we already have the place for the meeting?"

"The headquarters of the United Nations. Everyone will come," said the President.

"Good. I'll tell Erik Fenton about it. He is the one who has a direct contact with this being. This is the first time a civilian will be allowed to attend such a meeting," said General Rock.

Chapter 82

It was a long night and an equally long morning. Erik Fenton woke up with a little headache. It was around noon. He walked slowly like an old man into the bathroom, then down the stairs. The family was in the living room. Only Irina sat at the dining table staring into her mobile. She shouted "Dad," very pleased when she saw him. The mobile was unimportant. Her father was the most important thing in her life. The sons also rejoiced at his appearance.

"Good morning," he croaked out a little. His voice was not yet fully awake.

"How are you?" was asked.

"A little headache and my bones hurt, but whatever. A man has just these symptoms at a certain age. Disregarding those things, I'm still good as I can be."

"The way you fought, not even a younger man can hold a candle to you," Andy said. "Out of respect, we didn't touch your sword, although honestly, it itched in our fingers to cut through the air with it. It still lies there," and pointed to the ground.

Erik bent down and lifted it up. "Who wants to hold it," he asked.

"Me," the children said in unison.

Mikael was the oldest. He tried it first and sweated. "I am not a weakling, but this sword is simply too heavy. How could you use it so easily, father?" he asked.

"I also had trouble to lift it. Only by the power of the Nameless had I succeeded and spent many years handling it."

Andy and Irina tried. The sword was too heavy.

"I think I will put it aside now," he said and brought it to the cellar.

As soon as he was back up in the living room, front door rang. It was none other than Mr. Dumbler and General Rock.

"Am I disturbing you? Is it too early? Should I come back later? Or may I come in?" the general asked.

Helen Fenton cleared the way. "It's all right, even if I have so many questions. My husband is still a little beaten, but please do come in," and she close the front door behind him.

Mister Dumbler moved to his car and waited for the general to return.

"Long time no see," Fenton said.

"Yes," the general grinned," it has been quite a long time ago."

"Did something happen?" asked Erik.

"The meeting will take place tomorrow at the headquarters of the United Nations. I suspect it will be around noon. I will pick you up and fly you there earlier."

"I'm invited to join in?" Fenton asked in surprise. "What am I going to do there?"

"Yes. At the request of the President of the United States of America. You are the hero of the nation. He wants to get to know you and honor you for your deeds."

"I'm not sure," Erik replied and frowned.

"The Nameless one will be there and certainly wouldn't mind. That's how I believe it anyway."

"All right," said Erik Fenton. "I will go into the lion's den. Let's see what our friend wants to get rid of tomorrow. So far, I don't know anything. Maybe it's better that way."

"Good," said General Rock. "See you tomorrow," and said goodbye.

A few minutes later, Mister Dumbler drove the general to their next appointment.

"What is it?" Helen Fenton said. She knew Erik.

"I don't know. There will certainly be something coming that we didn't expect. The Nameless one will enlighten us tomorrow."

They spent the rest of the afternoon and evening together, because tomorrow was the end of the anticipation.

Chapter 83

In a soft voice, the Nameless man spoke to his crew, "Is the work done?"

"Yes," a voice whispered from the background and sounded lovely. "Everything will be ready for tomorrow."

"Good," meant the Nameless one. "I hope that mankind will understand what I have in mind."

Chapter 84

It was quiet in the quarter where the Fenton family was. A dog barked from somewhere. In between, you could hear the hissing and the fighting between two cats. A natural evening and night occurrence in the neighborhood. Erik rolled from one side to the other. Bathed in sweat, he dreamed of the Nameless. He had registered with him mentally. They communicated with each other. Erik told him where the meeting of the nations will take place. Before the Nameless man broke the contact, he revealed to Erik a part of what was coming to them. Of course, he kept quiet until the nameless tell the people. At that moment, Erik awoke and cried out his fear. The scream was heard all over the neighborhood. A few houses turned on their lights. Everyone was surprised by the disturbance of their night slumber. Helen was terrified and her children hurried into their parents' bedroom.

"Father," spoke Irina. "What happened? Are you alright?"

"Speak. Tell me please," Helen spoke in fear. She haven't seen Erik like that. Something must have happened. But what?

"I am afraid I cannot. I must not tell you," and struggled for air. He drank the glass of water on the bedside table. "Go to sleep, everyone. I apologize for interrupting your sleep. Now go," he said as he lay down. His breath was heavy. He calmed down after a few minutes and thought about the newly acquired knowledge.

The three left the bedroom in sorrow and left their parents behind. Helen grabbed her chest and breathed just as hard.

"Erik," she whispered "What happened? What have you got?"

Erik did not reply and only cried in secret. That was not a good sign. Truly not. Seeing that her husband will not disclose anything, she left him alone and watched him only from the side. At some point, her eyes closed and slept until morning.

The big day had begun. Erik got up and took a shower. Then, he squeezed himself into a suit and went to the dining table. Breakfast was already ready. Helen, the good soul of the house, had already prepared everything.

She looked at Erik and whistled through her teeth, "My, my! Look at that fine husband of mine."

"Thank you, my love," and looked at her with a sad look.

"Still disturbed?" she said and straightened his tie. He did not speak, but nodded.

"Turn on the TV after I leave. It's going to be broadcasted live," he said. "I beg you, no matter what happens, don't be afraid. Keep a cool head."

He stroked Helen's homemade jam on a toast and bit it. As soon as he was finished, it rang at the front door. A soldier stood in front of it.

"Mr. Fenton?"

"Yes?"

"General Rock sent me to pick you up. The helicopter is standing by the road. May I ask you to follow me?"

He took a look back. Helen and the three young adults stood with her. They looked after him with concern. He closed the front door behind him and followed the soldier with heavy steps. A short time later, he got on the helicopter and flew towards the place of the begrudged meeting.

Chapter 85

The glider of the spaceship started to move. It floated down and broke through the earth's atmosphere. Its destination was the high house. It was the place where the Nameless one was expected. On board with him were two more beings.

Chapter 86

Ted Gibbs was connected to the Division. He just got a message that an object had broken through the Earth's atmosphere. He was eagerly awaiting the arrival of this object on the roof of the UN building. The whole area was secured by the military. Countless fighter jets flew through the almost destroyed city. No mouse came through. The glider landed on the roof. General Rock stood and received the new arrivals. The three beings who came out surprised him. He had only expected the Nameless one, but who are the other two? It shuddered him when he saw these beings wrapped in cloths. One creature looked dried up, as if there was not a drop of water in the brown and sandy body while the other being was only a slippery moss. Tough drops separated from his body and clapped to the ground.

'Yuck,' the general thought. 'What the hell did we invite?'

The Nameless man turned around and spoke. "Do you always judge others so quickly who don't fit into your concept; those looking all different yet still saved your life?"

'He can read my mind,' the general thought, surprised. "No, I apologize. Please follow me," he said and accompanied these extraordinary guests into the great hall.

The room was quiet. The President of the United States spoke to those present. He praised Erik Fenton, who stood next to him and looked very embarrassed.

"We owe it to this man that mankind, these extraterrestrial invaders, have been destroyed. He deserves the highest honor we can give."

Through the thunderous applause, he shook Erik's hand.

"I thank you, Mr. President, and I am honestly embarrassed to receive this award but I am grateful," said Fenton.

The main door of the great hall was opened and the general escorting the three most important guests entered. The applause stopped. All eyes were on the beings who were walking towards the stage. Some of those present looked away in disgust. Others were very interested at these unique creatures. A whisper went through the rows.

"Please sit down and listen to what they have to say," the President said into the microphone on the speaker's desk.

After everyone sat down, some were still whispering. That was really extraordinary. The aliens will speak to them. The general brought them forward and stopped at the side. Ted Gibbs also stood there and was in charge of the security. The hall was also secured by many armed guards.

"It is my honor to welcome you here today," said the President. "Like everyone else, we are excited to hear what you have to say to us."

The Nameless man and the other two bowed and slowly the nameless stepped towards the lectern. His eyes looked into the questioning faces of the crowd. Erik Fenton stood next to the President and whispered to him. "It is better if we all sat down and no matter what happens, accept it."

"You know what this is about?" he asked in surprise.

Erik said nothing more and sat down on a free shell chair. The President, with countless thoughts and questions, sat down as well.

"Erik Fenton wants to give something to everyone," the Nameless man spoke to him.

He stood up briefly and spoke to those present. "Listen to him well. Do not interrupt him in his speech unless he permits it. That is all," and sat down again.

The speaker shone in a bright light and impressed those present very much. He took a look at the two other beings, nodded and was ready. This speech radiated all over the world. Everyone could follow it on the screen. Those who did not have a television set could receive it thru their smartphones, others with the radio, tablet or laptops. Many reporters also sat in the hall. Everyone wanted to know what this alien had to say. A deafening silence had broken out in the room.

"I gave myself the name...the Nameless," it started. "Only Mister Erik Fenton knows my real name and it will stay that way," and nodded to Erik.

"I will tell you many points of this story or speech. What you have experienced in the last few days was not just something that happened. It was pre-programmed a long time ago."

A quiet murmur went through the present.

"I was born as a malignant being and, with the help of Halley's comet, I transformed myself into this being which stands before you today. I was endowed with powers that are unimaginable. Before I arrived on Earth, I traveled through the vastness of space and discovered two different planets, whose leaders are standing with me today. They helped me to destroy my brother and the tide of enemies. They don't speak much, but they are asking for your help. The help to heal their two planets. Give them back their lives." The Nameless one took a pause.

He looked at the President and he asked, "What can we give you?"

"Water and Earth," came his answer.

"We can give you that. How much do you need?" asked the President.

"I will explain it to you later. For now, thank you for your support," the Nameless man said and looked at his companions.

"One leader comes from a planet that is consisted of more water than earth. It almost never rains and when it does, it rains very little. It is divided into two continents and governments. The ocean and the coral barrier rests in between. A wall was built on this. The wall sank again and again into the coral bank. Deep in the ocean, the most important food of the inhabitants gathered. They ate algae, fish and enjoyed the plankton that stuck to the wall. Above the walkable wall, the inhabitants work with scratching tools and so, they could harvest the food. As a reward for these gifts, they built temples and prayed to their water god.

The development of the planet was good, but then, the day came when everything changed. The population, from one side of the continent, exploded suddenly. More and more inhabitants and food became scarce. The government and powerful corporations forged their plans. Hate, envy, espionage and intrigue were spun and eventually hired soldiers to take everything. They sparked a war. By countless fire attacks against the other side and on the water, it began to evaporate. The inhabitants asked for the help of their water god, but their screams remained unheard. The aggressors used a different tactic. They poured dangerous substances, feces and much more into the water. That was a mistake. It killed the fish and the corals. The whole ecological water system collapsed. Not only for one side. Also, the other side got something off, because the wall opened again and again and the water flowed over. Now it was time to act.

One night, the attacked were on their way. Armed with water from underground springs, which were absolutely deadly, they went to the other side. The water was like an acid and they caused a bloodbath there. This went on until both sides gave up. Now they had to find a solution. A solution for a new life on the planet and they found it.

Together they researched, constructed special machines to make their lives easier. Some even for their future. Developed flying objects that catapulted them into space. Always on the lookout for water and found none. At some point it would become even less and then?

This evolution of decades had its price. Their bodies changed due to the polluted water. Likewise, through food. It became dry. So that they did not dry out, they stroked the water mixed with earth, as mud, to their bodies. You see the leader of these beings before you," and point with a movement at this and it bowed.

"The other being comes from a planet more made of earth than water. It wasn't like that before. There were forests and lakes everywhere. A whole planet full of plants. The best there ever was. But even here these beings failed. As on the other planet, there were corporations that abused these plants, the forests for their purposes. They also found out that under the earth's surface there were huge deposits of liquids that they needed for their material purposes. So, they pumped it off. When one cell was empty, they started with the next. As a result, the ground was no longer stable. It sank together. Huge holes were created.

The water from the lakes flowed into the holes and dried up in the ground. This planet began to crumble. The forests were cleared and soon there was only one desert left. The oxygen went back. The plants and everything edible became bad and spoiled. The critical point had almost come. They hoped for help from their forest god and faith. Nothing was heard. So, they sat down and talked and talked, but no one acted. Their bodies began to decompose. It became sandy and dried up. So, it began until a simple farmer came into town and opposed the government. He was willing to donate his money to build reasonable machines.

Machines to save the planet. Many inhabitants followed the example of the farmer and helped.

They worked on these perfect machines, but what they lacked was earth. Good soil to sow, new forests to grow and holes to fill. Simply everything. The end was almost there when I arrived and had to act. I promised to help them, but I also needed their help. With them I developed spaceships that they could bring water to life, the earth to plug the holes, on other planets. But even these did not have much to offer. They had to get along with the little they had. I left them and promised to come back when I discovered something. Water for both planets and earth in addition."

The Nameless one pointed to the other being with the sandy body and it bowed. A small pause arose. In spite of the air conditioning, it became warm to some listeners. They sweated and some men loosened their tie buttons. The whole world listened to the voice and story of the Nameless man. After a few moments it continued.

"I knew my brothers were after me because I had destroyed our homeland. I flew through space. That the Halley comet had already flown almost through the entire Milky Way system, I could guess that the earth was in a certain sector. Here I hid from my brothers. This planet had everything the others needed. Water, earth, oxygen. Simply everything!

I could have sent a message to both leaders. But read it and stay. My brothers would have intercepted them safely and would have landed here centuries ago. I didn't want that. So, I hid my spaceship, by the mountains, in a well camouflaged cave. Then I walked through a forest and laid my paws or paws, as you would ay, on the ground. I felt the soft moss and rubbed it. Equipped with my powers, I felt the earth pulsate. But after a few seconds I got a strong electric shock from the friction (electrostatic charge). I, who felt no fear, withdrew frightened. I had felt the future of this planet. I had to act and forged a plan. A dangerous plan with cunning and treachery. I now held the future in my hand, you would say. No matter how many losses there would be, it was about humanity. The salvation of the earth dwellers. My body began to tremble and my astral body, you call it that, detached itself from my body. As it already happened on the other two planets. I did not know how long I was in this state. My body lay on the ground and after a long time my spirit returned to it."

The Nameless one looked at those present. The countless questions were written on their faces.

"You are probably wondering where I had been."

A nod went through the rows.

"I am now picking up a topic that you will not like. Forgive me! Through the power I overcame the dimensions and sought help. Help, like my two companions here. I looked for your gods to whom you pray again and again. From Asia, via the Middle East and the rest of the world. I still let you believe, but in reality, I found no one. There was nothing. No existence. Nothing."

An outcry of indignation took place in this hall.

"How dare you say this in our faith, in our core values? You have no proof," the people in the room shouted. The outcry went through the whole world. One heard everywhere only:

"Blasphemy, kill this dog," and much more. Head shaking and horror was the reaction.

"Calm down and sit down again," said the Nameless man.

Slowly calm came again in the hall and he continued. Every now and then one heard a clearing of the throat. That got under the skin of many.

"As already said. I found no indication of an existence, except, something hold me back to explore more," he took a break "in an intermediate realm. It was the Nordic deities Odin and Thor. None of you had thought or prayed of them. They had fallen into oblivion. They were perfect warriors and exactly what I needed. They were waiting for their last warrior. That was Erik, the Viking. But he stayed away from them because he was still needed. Used for the fight against my evil brothers.

The gods could not enter into eternity, a further stage to completion, and thus waited for their time. I forged this plan with them, as well as with Erik, the Viking, and it looks like it worked out. They helped you to destroy my brother and the other hostile, vicious creatures. Faced them with simple weapons. The first time I set them a trap. My brothers thought I was on earth. That was so, but only as a spirit. My body had dissolved. They followed a cry which immediately led them here to kill me. That went wrong. Only one brother survived and I let him go. He disappeared into the infinity of the universe.

I changed back from spirit to body and left you. But read my spirit and power to one man. This is Erik Fenton. Through him I could follow world events. I saw him, as well as Erik, the Viking, through the centuries with his descendants, through their eyes. I flew through space and went back to the two planets. Here all their spaceships mobilized and flew towards the earth. It took time. According to your calendar it was more than twenty-five years.

However, we were able to open a black hole to cover the distances faster. Now plan two started. I knew that my enemy brother would come again and I set my trap here too. He was not alone and gathered all the enemy and most vicious creatures in this Milky Way around him. He wanted total annihilation and above all, my death. You know the rest."

The Nameless one looked at those present. No words. There was peace. A calm before the storm. Erik Fenton knew this and waited for this moment.

Chapter 87

While the Nameless spoke, a call for Ted Gibbs hummed through the silent mobile. He walked to the side and heave a breath before answering.

"What's the matter?" he asked, in whispering tone. "I hope it's important."

"Sir, something's wrong. We've detected a strong radiation. This is coming from the bright spaceship. They are surrounding the entire Earth's atmosphere and slowly descending on different areas."

"What did you say?! Damn it! I knew something was off here," and hung up. With a fuming head, he gave a sign to the security personnel. They slowly lifted their weapons and pointed it against the Nameless one and the two other beings.

Chapter 88

The President of the United States cleared his throat before he got up and spoke.

"That was a detailed report, which we heard. Thank you," and nodded, for respect. "I'm sure everyone still has questions for you. Why us? Was it just about water and earth? Why did you bring all these enemies to us? I mean, the enemy has been defeated for us, which we greatly appreciate, but the cities are left in ruins and many people have died."

"When I saw the future then, I knew I had to act. I am a good being who wants to give you the best, so does my two companions. The earth was the perfect place to destroy the balance and eliminate all evil. That is why I wanted them to come here. You are a war-obsessed creature who have not changed with age. Throughout the centuries, I've seen what you've done. You have built your temples, shrines and churches with a faith in one or more deities. Which is absolutely your right, if you believe in it. My two companions have discarded their faith and have been able to evolve. There are no temples or anything else left on their planet. They used their time better than with just praying. They dedicated themselves to the welfare of their population. Meanwhile, you, earth dwellers, are obsessed with starting pointless thousand wars. Thus, going to lengths of travelling to other countries killing men, children and women, whom are either being salvaged, enslaved or sexually assaulted. You have written it all in your records yet no one wants to admit your nature. Mostly this, in the name of your gods, whom I suppose is only a tool you use for material gain and justifying your manslaughtering actions".

"That's enough!" the President and all the others present shouted with loud voices.

Countless murmurs have echoed the place. However, a halting outcry stopped the world from their tracks with the next words of the Nameless One.

"I. Am. Not. Finished. Yet. Sit. Down," said the Nameless One with a deeper, threatening and commanding voice.

An uncontrollably tremendous power equipped the bodies of everyone, forcing them to sit back down to their sits. They can't resist but follow the Nameless' order.

The Nameless sighed before continuing, "We feel your anger towards us. We feel that after this declaration, we are no longer welcome. I see that your soldiers have raised their weapons against us. A sign of insecurity, of malaise; ravaging fear of what might come. I have come to thank you for giving us water and earth. We could have taken it without asking. But our decency and honor forbids us to do so."

A woman reporter from the middle called over to him. "How much is it? How much water and dirt do you need after all these insults?"

"Fresh water, Ocean water and Earth Soil. Specifically, three quarters each of your planet."

Many cried out, others held their hands in front of their mouths while others had their jaw wide open. The shock was deep.

"Then we would have nothing at all! Everything would be gone. What are we supposed to live on," a reporter shouted through the hall and the members of the United Nations also wanted to know.

"Through my words and my power, it will take a few seconds and everything will change. The end of everything. The new beginning will ring in," said the alien speaker. "Let me explain."

That was too much for those present. The President of the United States gave the order, "Rain Fire."

The guards wanted to open fire, but nothing happened. All weapons had jams. None worked.

"As I said before," said the Nameless man, unaffected with what the President said. "You are very destructive inhabitants. It is always the same thing over and over. First shoot your firearms on everything that you disagree with, then think of the consequences. However, in the end, you don't really care. You only care for yourselves. Put down your weapons and listen to my words."

The whole world watched this spectacle. Terribly shocked as they followed the events in the hall.

"You must have noticed something in the last few days. Our smaller spaceships in your orbit confused all your minds and technology. They scanned the entire surface of the Earth. In addition, your computer system was hacked. That was me collecting all the data from you and from every inhabitant of the earth. There are over eight hundred spaceships in orbit awaiting for my signal."

"What is going to happen now," asked the President of the United States in a frightened voice.

It was also not good for the others present. The Nameless man revealed his secret.

"Point one. The radiation came out a few minutes ago from my spaceship and covered the earth, and all weapon systems were switched off. Nothing will work anymore. No weapon in this world can fire a shot. None! In exactly 10 minutes, all enemy flying objects and weapon systems of the aggressive humans will dissolve into nothing. Just like your nuclear and war weapons. This means that there will be no more wars. Your soldiers and law enforcers will become unemployed. Point two. Today, the gates will open in all prisons. All will be free for a while. I will give these criminal persons two days to meet with their families. After that, it will be different. Point three. Criminal institutions and associates will be gone."

There was a short break before he continued.

"You have exploited the earth. Corporations have pumped the oil out of the earth and left many empty holes. Gas was extracted.

The oceans of the world are heavily polluted by oil and other pollutants. Does this sound familiar to you?"

"Enough," spoke a man from the row. "That may be true, but we still don't know what to expect from everything that you said."

"The end," said the Nameless man, taking a deep breath. "You have brought it this far. All of you. In exactly Six months, Eighteen days, Thirteen hours and Seven minutes, the Earth will be no more. It will go down and with it, all of you. The ground will open, all water will seep into the ground, nuclear reactors will explode and contaminate everything. There is no escape."

Those were the words of the Nameless One. The shock was very deep. Too deep in the minds of the people. They took their time and looked into each other's frightened faces.

In the hall, those present sweat the sweat of death. The whole world stood still. Now, everyone knew what was coming. People ran everywhere, screaming in all directions. Some threw themselves on the floor and cried. Others ran into the churches and prayed. The chaos was perfect. Many kept a cool head because they couldn't change anything anyway and kept looking at the screens.

"That's why all the enemies who came and were born to this planet had no future. Whether they destroyed it or by nature, it didn't matter. So, I'll clean the entire Milky Way from all evil creatures."

"What's the next step then?" asked one member of parliament.

"Now I'll give you ten minutes to think. I offer you the future that I am building nicely. However, according to my rules and my law, accept it or go under. Your choice."

These were the hard words of the Nameless. Horror was written in their faces. Dry moist swallowed their saliva. The deputies, statesmen and women sat in their seats, bathed in sweat. It began with a whisper and then with loud murmurs. Everyone was talking in confusion.

"What does it want to do to us? What is his plan? Subjugation of humankind? The Nameless one is dangerous. What can we do against him?"

Erik Fenton stayed in the background. He just listened to the nonsense of these statesmen and women. No one had understood what the Nameless man really wanted A perfect world. A peaceful future. Peace returned to the hall.

"What is your decision?" asked the Nameless man.

"We have no answer. It is either stay here and perish or submit to you. We have no choice. You get to decide our fate anyways," said the President of the United States of America.

"Yes. It's a life choice to make, and I'll do it for you. In the last twenty-five years, both leaders have built everything for you. You will be resettled there."

There was an even more confused outcry from mankind.

"Besides, I can't save them all. As already said, no criminal elements will be tolerated. Nor are there any animal tormentors and desecrators who kill for fun, nor are there those who watches and enjoys it. For example, be it at a bullfight, dogs hanging alive on the trees or geese tearing off the feathers on the living body. Keeping animals in cages to get a good coat. There will also be no more zoos, as all animals will live in limited but free wildlife.

In two days, with my power, almost half of humanity will be eliminated. The other good people will get an electronic implant on the back of their heads. All your personal memories will be stored in it and can be passed on to the next generation. If you refuse to accept it, you will remain on earth and die with it.

The water and the dirt will be picked up by my spaceships in orbit in one week and brought to the two planets. The two leaders of the planets have built special machines. Through a special process, they can reduce it in size and transport larger quantities. In their homeland, everything is enlarged again. All strong land, air and water animals, microbes and insects will be also taken along".

A clap from a reporter in the background briefly interrupted the speech of the Nameless man.

He had hit his neck with his right hand. "Damn mosquitoes. I hope this alien won't bring them," he whispered to himself.

"I can reassure you," the Nameless man addressed the man. "Annoying, useless and dangerous insects will not be on the list."

He thanked him and raised his hand to greet him. There was a red spot on the palm of his hand.

"I'm sure there are many open questions for me, which I will explain to you later."

"What does our future look like?" asked one of the participants from the hall.

"First, you'll reside in the two planets. There, the dwellings are already ready for you. There you will learn how to deal with each other peacefully. There will only be acceptance of the color of your skin and your faith. Should anyone not accept this, it will be eliminated. So, there will be no more hatred or war of religions, as it has been here on earth for thousands of years and still is. You will learn to deal with the new technology, medicine and much more. Everything will become easier. As I said, the earth will not be habitable. This will be so for twenty years until the earth has recovered from the radioactivity. Then both leaders will come back to earth and restore it to its original state. We have scanned it. Every stone, every mountain, every sea and ocean will be the same as before. Every sight will be put back in its original place. The water and the earth will be brought back reproduced.

There will be only one currency. Everyone works for the good of all mankind. The perfect plan, I will explain to you later as well. The earth will blossom again to life and will become the largest trading center of the Milky Way. There are so many planets out there that are inhabited. Many aliens will come and trade. Treat them well, with dignity and respect. Those who do not abide by it, be it on your side or on the other, will be eliminated. There is also another problem you have to face.

After the volcanoes are extinct and the lava has cooled, many caves will form. With your faith, you may build your churches, shrines and minarets in them. There must be no visible elements on the surface. The evaluators, in unknown other galaxies, do not know it and will perceive it as a threat. I ask you to note this."

"There is something wrong," one said. "You have said that all evil is destroyed. So, we are threatened after all and cannot defend ourselves."

"You are protected by the two leaders of the planets. That is guaranteed here, in this Milky Way. But what is outside of it, the unknown? I will be there, I will look around and I will travel far."

The Nameless one looked into the faces of those present. Everyone was silent.

"By my power, I will send an impulse to earth. Then, all the people who will be eliminated will be on the street. In the next two days, build the pits for the dead. That is all I have to say as of the moment."

The Nameless one and its two companions left the room. With the glider, they flew to the spaceship. There was thick air in the hall. Nobody knew what to do.

Erik Fenton stood up and spoke to the President. "It is better if you all go home. There is nothing more to say."

"Yes, I believe that, too," said one of the others.

Most whispered, others remained silent. Everyone followed his or her thoughts. The hall emptied itself eventually. Erik Fenton was flown home by General Rock.

"What will come our way?" the general asked during the flight.

Fenton looked at him from the side.

"Paradise. You will retire, enjoy the evening of your life and drink a cool beer. Some unemployed people do that, don't they?" grinned Erik Fenton.

He nodded his head. "Maybe two beers, too. Let's see."

"That's what I like about you, General. We should finally relax."

Erik Fenton and the family enjoyed that wonderful evening with food and drinks. Later, they went into the garden and looked silently up at the stars. Everybody was thinking about the future, because it was only written in the stars.

The End.

Epilogue

Erik Fenton died of natural causes five days before the Earth went down. His ashes were taken to his new home. By his agreement and through the power of the Nameless, he slipped through a gap that was opened for him into the realm of the Vikings. He left his remaining strength to his children, who knew nothing about it.

Till this day, the Nameless continues to watch over them.

Books by BELLAVISTA

The Warrior from the Past
THE AWAKENING
PAST AND PRESENT

The Nameless
THE AWAKENING
THE LAST FIGHT

Other English Novels
THE BAR

Novels in Other Languages
DER AUSERWÄHLTE (Pub. 2006)